THE
THROUGH

by A. Rafael Johnson

Johnson, A. Rafael
The Through / A. Rafael Johnson

Published by Jaded Ibis Press.
http://www.jadedibispress.com

 JADED IBIS PRESS

For Dad and his fractured fairy tales, 1946 - 2016.

The
Through

The Nappy-Headed Doll

Adrian developed too early. Men began to notice her when she turned ten and still played with dolls. Adrian took a pair of rounded school scissors and cut the curly hair off her black Barbie.

"You nappy headed," she declared. "You so ugly."

Adrian spent a week painstakingly weaving straight blonde hair into the dolls short locks, but the plastic wouldn't hold. The hair fell off. She tried to glue the hair straight onto the doll's head, but dry glue drips made the doll even uglier, deformed from a hidden cancer bubbling to the surface. Adrian threw the doll into the back of her bedroom closet but couldn't sleep, so she moved the doll under her bed and stayed up all night thinking about her, then finally buried the doll in her backyard under the shade of her mother's banana leaf palm in lower New Orleans, dirty, crying, scratching the dirt of her mother's garden with a cheap trowel. A man noticed her.

Adrian remembered this day as the day she met her ice twin, a frozen soul who orbited the same small brown body gasping under the man from behind the fence. One twin cried and sweat. She bled. She stank. She clutched. She hurt. She panted and drooled. The other, the ice twin, created a cool world of crystalline perfection in a high place full of majestic glaciers and frozen plains where nothing changed, nothing hurt, and nothing sweat. When the ugly twin ran into trouble, often, always, she begged her icy sister for advice and the twin always answered. The ice twin loved giving advice. Every time the man returned the ice twin told her sister how they had no one but each other, how their mother would never believe them, how to shut the fuck up, how to talk pretty, how to do things the man liked so she wouldn't get in trouble, until her thoughts formed an unending floe spread through Adrian's heart to the tips of her fingers and toes and hair. *That's it*, she said, *stand closer, you're so dirty, don't eat that, stupid, don't cut where they can see, stupid, say I love you too Uncle Marcel, I'll always be yours, say it, just say it.*

Adrian, the twin Adrians, grew and did things twins do. They finished sixth grade with perfect attendance. They auditioned for low budget commercials and parade floats. They posed for swimsuit photos. They attended college, dropped out, and took jobs wherever they could find: restaurants, retail, even a job delivering donuts to senior citizen homes and drunken frat parties at 5 in the morning. They lived life in New Orleans: parties, men, women, parades, church, food, and very little money. The ice twin never gained an ounce, never changed her hair, never got over excited about a new dress or a cute boy at church. Adrian changed, and then noticed men noticing her more as her hips got larger.

Make them happy, the twin said.

But Marcel wouldn't notice her, not anymore, no matter what Adrian promised or how she begged. She was too old, too mouthy, too fat, too much.

"You always want attention," her mother said. "Stop lying."

"Bitch it never happened, you hear me?" Marcel said.

Lying flew up Adrian's fingers, up her arm. *Bitch* jumped into her ears and slid down frozen canals, fading into the deepest recess, the darkest crevice. Together, the words slid into her frozen chest wall, lightless, loveless, hopeless, forgotten but sharp and grating and hot every second of every minute of every hour of every day.

With encouragement from her icy sister, Adrian developed her anti-gravity stance. Her hips grew but weighed less. She floated across the broken sidewalks, barely touching the ground, up stoop stairs, across porches. Adrian preferred gliding along rails instead of riding streetcars. Boyfriends and girlfriends came and left. Ben held on longer than most but the twin knew everyone left her, just like Marcel. After one intense night, Ben lay panting and sweaty on the sheets. Adrian sat quietly, knees hugged to her chest.

"Did you?" Ben trailed off.

No, always no.

"You got ice water in your veins," he said.

Ben complained: Adrian held back, Adrian hid things, Adrian gave him the cold shoulder. She'd heard it all before. Ben was right and wrong. Adrian gave everything, Adrian had no secrets, Adrian walked arm in arm with her twin every day and night, naked with her clothes on. The twin froze Adrian under a permafrost no one could thaw, keeping her sister, her doll, her blood, sweat, rage and pain buried under miles of thick ice, preserved, protected, untouchable, until memories become fossils left for future archeologists to unearth after a cataclysm, after the planet flew too close to the sun, after Adrian and her twin and her mother and Marcel, all dust for millennia, slipped the grip of gravity and floated into space—motes shedding the last warmth of the sun as they drifted apart.

On August 29, the day of howling wind, the day of bloody water, the day of trees detonating like bombs, the day of coffins busting from crypts to make space for the living, the day turned night, the day of a storm so monstrous and terrible that Adrian thought the world must end, the ice twin clamped down. She tried. Adrian screamed when unseen objects crashed into her mother's house. The ice twin froze the floor beneath Adrian's feet, but it was too much water, too much. Their shotgun house flooded. Adrian scrambled into the attic, panicked, until the twin said, *there stupid. Right there!* and Adrian found a gap-toothed saw.

On the roof, heat, and the sound of dripping water. Nothing else made a sound, not a bird, not a breath of wind. The city drowned. While the ugly twin wept in shocked silence, the ice twin grew colder. She drew the heat of the drowned city into her body and endured. She could freeze the entire Ward if she had to, the entire city. *I shall remake in my image*, the ice twin thought. *Freeze the bones. No one will ever hurt us again.* She imagined herself as the new New Orleans, with every house, every wrought-iron fence, every sycamore tree, every blade of grass, every drop of water from her sister's tears to the Mississippi frozen and still.

The long-buried, nappy-headed doll floated up from under the uprooted banana palm tree. She wasn't supposed to. Adrian heard a great glacier crack and crumble and saw her ice twin for the first time. Adrian knew of her twin since the day at the fence, had imagined her, listened to her, felt her cold presence, but until this moment had never seen her. She looked like Adrian imagined she would look if Adrian developed late, or on time. Her lips, skin, hair, teeth were translucent blue-black, as if she was cut from the heart of an iceberg far off the southern coast of Africa. Vapor steamed around her body, and water condensed on her cold skin. She stood in her element, fierce and confident.

The nappy-headed doll bobbed along the surface, carried along by a swift current. The twin embraced her sister. She leaned in and said something Adrian could not hear. Then the ice twin ran across the roof, dove into the rancid flood, and swam after the doll they buried all those years ago. Adrian heard another crack. Her sister's foot fell off and dissolved. Another crack and her left arm was gone. Her sister floundered, melted, grew smaller. Could ice drown in water? Coated in filth, the ice twin gave one last lunge and captured the doll with a melting hand. Adrian cried out. Her sister grinned in triumph, then melted into a brief cold puddle. Adrian collapsed, screaming.

Days later, rescuers arrived and took her, still screaming, she couldn't stop, to a place where Adrian could cool down and forget what happened. Adrian forgot herself instead. Adrian forgot her sister and her mother and her home. Forgot her pink shotgun house; forgot *Fire on the Bayou* warped under the window. Forgot her chain fence with the beads and her sign: *Take One Have Fun. Take Two, Voodoo!* Forgot her mother's garden and her little dog peeing on the banana tree and the green parrots sleeping in the hibiscus. Forgot crack-a-lack sidewalks. Forgot her spot on the porch where she rubbed the paint off from sitting, saying "hey baby hey mama hey fine man hey playa naw Mister ain't no Adrian at this number but if you leave your name I'm sure she come down and pay soon she get off work." Forgot her church, her choir, her pew, her priest, her sick-and-shut-ins. Forgot Mrs. Emma with her bad legs and a hundred pictures of grandkids been dead for twenty years. Forgot St. Francis. Forgot Hubig's. Forgot water. Forgot cutting herself. Forgot Lake Pontchartrain, forgot the Orleans Canal and the 17th St. Canal and the Mississippi and the Gulf. Forgot laughing, smiling, lemonade. Forgot giving directions to tourists. Forgot her job at the casino and her other job at the store and forgot paying rent late. Forgot her mother. Forgot mama say if the big one come get me out and forgot about mama and forgot about forgetting. Forgot smelling her shoes rot off her feet in the heat. Forgot hot black grit itching under her toenail. Forgot Marcel trapped between a car and a fence, water inching up over his chest and neck, over his face. Forgot Ray Nagin and Governor Landrieu and George W. Bush. Forgot the Coast Guard and FEMA and the Royal Mounted Canadian Police. Forgot Sean Penn in his boat and Fats in his house. Forgot reporters. Forgot rumors, looters, shooters. Forgot houses marked in red X paint after the Angel of Death already come and gone. Forgot the Dome, forgot going thirsty until thirsty bucked like a wild animal dying inside her chest. Forgot licking sweat off her hands and crying until the tears ran out and a man yelling "what the fuck you wasting water for?" Forgot the school bus to Houston, forgot the Harris County Psychiatric Center. Forgot them damn questions, forgot them damn pills. Forgot the intake form, forgot she ain't got no address no more, forgot crying again and there still ain't no tears coming out ain't nothing down there but a dry well. Forgot singing in the kitchen before the sun came up, forgot making collards for family reunion, forgot old photos under wax paper.

Adrian felt like a piece of nothing left behind. Felt like a ghost, floating, like if she just let go a little the world would fly away and leave her behind in the sunlight. Might be nice to float, no water, no sound, just sunlight. No feelings. Adrian wasn't numb. She just didn't feel anything. She forgot. Like the time she got beaned by the Orpheus Krewe. Just a little kid then and the beads knocked her to the sidewalk. But Adrian forgot how to feel, so she remembered the blood dripping down her forehead like it was a show she'd seen on TV, remembered stich-itch, remembered the whooping for getting stains on her clothes even though it wasn't her fault but didn't she know not to stand so close? She remembered the scar across her temple but it never hurt anymore.

Adrian wondered about her twin. The doctors told her to forget her twin. The nurses gave her pills and more pills with water. The chipped ice in her cup was her sister's body. The water was her blood. Disgusted, she threw the cup at the nurse. *Blasphemer.* Horrified, Adrian tried to scoop the ice from the floor with her bare hands.

"I forgot," she wailed. "I forgot, I forgot."

If ice could feel, would it feel like her? Nothing, just there, doing its thing, just getting its drink on, not even alive? Yes, exactly. No loyalty, no help thy mother and thy sister, no running, no charity, no floating cars. She wasn't angry. Adrian was post-anger. She flowed past Bill O'Reilly and Geraldo on the TV and past the nurses asking her again if she needed apple juice or a blanket or felt like talking with the doctor. Even when Adrian said no thanks yes please fuck you bitch whatever she just said it. A dead thing with breath. Weightless. Adrian wasn't even in the hospital. The real Adrian melted away during the flood. She would have gone anywhere but here. Her twin could travel to the bottom of the ocean, or to the polar cap where she would feel right at home. The ice twin would never mistake fucking for love and would never feel sorry for her sister for living in a hospital and drinking apple juice from a box.

A poster hung by the window next to her bed: a blonde woman stood on top of a snowy mountain, arms raised in celebration. Adrian could change into snow if she wanted, light and beautiful. She would fall over the city, scatter into the streets, the parks, into the bayou across the highway. Adrian felt an irresistible urge to break the window and leap, to dive down into those waters. Her sister lived in that bayou. Adrian knew it. She almost saw her face under the dark water and smiled for the first time in a long time, waved, and remembered other water, muddy hot water up to the roof, and remembering shook something aloose inside both Adrians, gurgling, choking, sputtering, sucking, shattering the calm waters.

A cold, dead voice yammered, 'you mine little mama you mine you mine.'

Adrian fled through the building like a scared little ghost and stood on the roof, arms raised in celebration over the sprawling city and the small bayou. None of it was hers. Pain sealed her off. She almost liked it. She wanted to let it all go and fade into nothingness. No life and death and struggles, no broken city full of broken children. Just nothing. Simple nothing.

"No pearly fucking gates," she thought. "I don't need this shit. And no harps. And no blues. No beat. I don't want nothing. I want to die and see nothing, hear nothing, feel, taste, smell, know nothing. Nothing."

The low clouds parted and a ship, an old wooden sailing ship, flew down and docked next to the rooftop. The crescent moon shone dimly down, illuminating masts and spars with no sails, a scarred deck, and hatches leading below. A gangplank extended itself from the ship's side to the rooftop, and a woman sang a song Adrian heard as a small child.

When she calls you better follow the sun
When she calls you better run, run, run

Adrian tried to board but her feet refused to move. She didn't know the words to her song. She struggled to speak and even massaged her jaw, but only produced a humiliating stutter for her city drowned dead, for her house and her street and her people, for her sister, for blood red grooves dug into her palm, for drowned mothers who could not find their children even from Heaven, for thirst.

ADRIAN

When the Moon Turns Red With Blood

.

I'm going to say something and get it out of the way. When I was a little girl, Uncle Marcel took me for a space. He's not my blood uncle, just an old friend of Mama's who used to hang around the house. It doesn't matter. I know now what he did was wrong and all, but I don't remember much. He liked the little noises I made. I wasn't violated. It wasn't rape. I wasn't sexual before him, so it's not like I understood something was wrong. I mean it hurt but wasn't wrong. I told my mother we were in love and going to have babies, and she slapped the shit out of me and called me a liar. Said I just wanted attention. It doesn't matter.

When we converted the top floors of the old Tuscaloosa National Bank into our offices, I'd tell Ben that I needed to supervise or take measurements again, any excuse really, then drive across the river from our little house in Northport into downtown Tuscaloosa, park, walk past the customers waiting to get into the Italian place downstairs, unlock the door, walk upstairs to the top floor, and lie down on the floor. I'd let the sweat of the day soak into the sawdust until I felt dry again. Ben loves to live with the windows open in this humidity and I just can't. Swimming, humidity, water, I just can't. If I could live without water, I would. I don't want to see it, listen to it, or feel it on my skin. I turn off the water when I shower. Just enough to get the soap working, then enough to take it off again. Ben thinks I'm being water-conscious. He's not wrong, but he's not right.

Before this office, we worked out of our homes or online. We met clients for lunch to talk business, sometimes here in Tuscaloosa, or at the country club in Northport. One of our wealthier clients knew someone who knew someone and suddenly we were offered this space to renovate into an office. The first time I came in here, a funny looking bird flew through a broken window and landed on an old desk right in front of me. *Cheeper-Cheeper Tape, Cheeper-Cheeper Tape*, it said and then flew off. I expected it to flutter and fly around the room, but it flew right out the way it came. The bird dropped an iridescent blue feather on the desk. I didn't remember it having blue feathers. After that, every time I came to the office, I'd find something left here for me. A pretty feather, a glass marble, a perfectly preserved dragonfly. I kept them all in a box in my desk. Good luck I guess.

And our cat. She wandered inside during a tense day. The inspector discovered a crack in one of out the steel support beams, so we had to hire a welder. He climbed up there, then came back down and said he wasn't sure the beam could be repaired. Me and my partners—Alice, Gloria, and Edward— debated on whether to try the repair (costly, might not work) or stop before we invested too much money. We were tied – Gloria and I for repairing, Edward and Alice for stopping. Then I heard a noise by my feet. I looked down and saw a tiny gray cat with a white stripe down her face. She looked like the cat version of me not too long ago, young and half-starved. I reached down and picked her up. She jumped into my arms and fell asleep.

"Well," Edward said, "There's our tiebreaker." We hired the welder. I took Free Cookie home and found Ben on the couch. I never knew writers watched so much TV.

"Hey," I said.

"Hey babe," he said, without looking up.

"We have a guest," I said, holding up the cat.

"A cat?" Ben said. "What's her name?"

"I don't know. I just found her at the office."

"Well, you found her, you name her," Ben said. "That's a rule."

"Oh really?"

"Really."

I thought about naming her after the restaurant under the office, but I never liked their food. Everyone here raves about it, but I'm from a city that understands food better than any other place on Earth. We invented the muffuletta, andouille sausage, dirty rice. My memory flew out the window and landed in my mother's dining room for Sunday dinner. Shrimp creole over white rice, potato salad, bread, and ice cream for dessert. I brought out a bottle of orange soda and placed it on the table. Mama wore a white sundress with red roses and a red rose in her hair. She looked so beautiful. My sister reminded me to get the ice.

"You brought the ice baby? That's a good girl," Mama said.

I didn't have anything special to leave at the table, and I froze. I couldn't speak. I shook my head violently until the memory left me.

Ben and the cat stared at me. "Are you alright?" Ben asked.

"Fine," I said. "Thought I had to sneeze."

The cat meowed at me. She knew I was lying.

You're right, I said silently. I shouldn't lie to Ben, but if he knew, he'd leave me. They'd all leave me. They all leave me.

"We probably shouldn't name her until we're sure she's a stray," Ben said. "We don't want to get attached and then find out she's some little kid's pet."

"Right," I said. "I'll put up some flyers."

Before I lived with Ben, I assumed that towns didn't really have main streets called Main Street. That seemed too obvious, like the time Kim Butler ran for Mayor with a picture of herself on a French Quarter set instead of in the actual French Quarter. The sidewalks are too even and the streets are too clean. That's what living in Northport feels like, like I'm acting in movie set in a small town, rather than living in an actual small town. We got the trendy nail salons, gift shops for baby showers and bachelorette parties, a yarn shop, and an art gallery on the corner, plus a scattering of houses before the street ends near the railroad trestle. People come here to take photos all the time, weddings, prom, all that. My favorite place is a bakery in the alley behind Main. When I can, I drop by and chat with the baker. She's funny and warm, and her coffee is good. Not the liquid-heart-attack regular coffee I came up with, but leaving home means leaving home. You can't get New Orleans coffee nowhere else. At the bakery, kids get free cookies. I suppose that's where I got the idea to name her Free Cookie. Everybody wants a free cookie.

As I taped Lost Cat flyers in the windows, I spotted a woman walking towards our place near the end of the street. She wore pink yoga shorts and a matching shirt of some tight material, maybe Lycra. She moved well, but her hair was styled for an older woman. More elegant than anything else. Hair for her own sake, not trying to attract a man. At first, I assumed she was just another jogger headed for the track along the river. But something about her seemed familiar, something in her back, her stride, the way she held her fingers as she walked, as if she inscribed the air.

She walked past our house without pausing. I don't know why I expected her to pause. I looked through our window. Ben was still sitting on the couch. I didn't see our new cat (in my heart, I knew) but she might have still been eating, or taking a nap in the kitchen window. I don't know why I did what I did next. I stuffed the leftover flyers and tape into our mailbox and followed the woman. She headed down to the jogging track and turned left. Left? The track ran right, clockwise, past the railroad trestle at the end of town, back to the softball fields in the park, and from there I don't know. I don't run unless I have to. Ben runs clockwise. Everyone here runs clockwise. That's what I mean about Northport being a movie. In real life, people run every which way, not in the same direction.

The woman walked straight at an old section of town Ben calls the Through. I think he's the only one who does. The area used to be a black neighborhood, but it's just a vacant lot now. There are no buildings left for a haint to haunt, but if one popped out of the pokeweed berries and said *how you be baby*, I'd say *awrite*.

Chickweed sprawled in circles across the ground, along long stems of green leaves with tiny white flowers on the end. Each plant made a circle of flowers, beautiful as a tarnished crown. Closer to the river, blue and lavender morning glories climbed the bridge pilings. The woman walked up to the chain link fence that blocked off a section of the river. She touched the fence with her palms and pushed. A rectangular section of chain-link fell away perfectly. She picked up the fence and set it to the side. Then, she walked through the fence towards a small hill. I wanted to follow her through, but how obvious would I be?

She'd be like, *what are you doing here?*

And I'd be like, 'what are *you* doing here?'

I couldn't follow her. This was crazy. I was about to turn around and go back when she turned around and I saw my mama's face. All the breath left my body. I thought this can't be real, mama's dead, mama died, she can't be this woman walking around. The woman stretched out her hand and the chickweed flowers grew under my feet and carried me to her. I knew her, every line on her face, every pore, the way she held her head, as if she was my own mother. She was my own mother. She took my hand. With a quick slice, she scratched my palm open but I didn't even move. My palm bled and something painful wiggled inside the cut. A cicada emerged, covered in bloody mud. The cicada dug its claws into my palm, then began pulsing. The shell grew and shrank in waves, then split open. A new cicada emerged from the old husk, opened its green wings, and flew away like an ember from a fire.

The woman, my mother, touched my face. I couldn't even cry. Then she said, "Cicada keep the time, hear?"

I nodded. The husk collapsed into dust. Chickweed flowers grew under my feet again and before I knew what, they set me down on the far side of The Through, right next to our house.

I looked around. No one seemed to think anything unusual or strange had happened. My hand began to throb. I looked at my palm. Mama had cut me in a long, diagonal slash. It bled less than before, but was still clotted with mud. I held my hand high to slow the bleeding and walked back inside.

"Hey hon—what happened to your hand?" Ben asked from the couch.

"Nothing," I said. "I fell."

Ben jumped up and grabbed my hand. "That looks deep," he said. "Maybe we should get you some stitches?"

Part of me wanted to close that slash forever, but I couldn't know if that cicada was the only one inside me. If my palm closed and another cicada tried to emerge, where would it go? My mouth, my ears? Would I sit down and pee green insects? The image made me giggle. "No, I'll just clean it off and wrap it," I said.

Ben looked like he was going to say something else, but then he just closed his mouth and said, "Okay."

He probably thought I giggled at him but he needs to understand my life ain't all about anyone but me.

In the bathroom, I looked at myself in the mirror. People tell me I'm beautiful but all I see is a collection of parts that never fit together. Large, almond-shaped eyes. Clear skin like masala in chocolate. Big mouth with too many teeth. No hips. Kinky hair, which takes for-fucking-ever to style. I used to perm, but it's too much trouble arguing with Ben about it. He's one of those back-to-the-motherland brothers who thinks Africa never saw a fashion magazine. Not a full-on Hotep but definitely showing some Hoteppish tendencies. All talk, no progress.

The water stung hard. I patted my hand dry, then looked through the medicine cabinet for something to cover it with. We didn't have a bandage large enough, so I wrapped my hand in gauze. The slash only bled a little.

I found Ben in the kitchen, pouring a beer from a can into a blue-rimmed glass.

"Pour me one?" I asked.

"Take this," Ben said, then opened another beer for himself. I held up the glass to drink, but noticed a splash of blue light on the wall, caused by the late afternoon sun shining through the rim of my glass. "Haint blue," I said.

"What's that?" Ben asked.

"That color." I pointed to the wall. "Haint blue."

"What's a 'haint blue'?"

"Your people never told you about haint blue?"

"If I knew I wouldn't ask," he said, sipping his beer.

Ben tells me his parents came from the South, but it seems like they ran from the South and left the best parts behind. They taught him about the Klan and Emmet Till, but forgot haints and sweet potato pies. The first time I cooked one, Ben's face lit up like a little boy. He's cute that way.

"Haints are people. They were people. Now they're ghosts that can't move on to the next life. Haint blue," I said as I took another sip, "is the color we painted porch ceilings to scare them off."

Without warning, a pipe burst under the kitchen sink. Water spouted out from the cabinets and flooded the floor.

Blood suddenly soaked my bandage, leaving a long red stain across the gauze.

"Shit!" Ben said, as he ran into the back room to find a wrench. I hurried into the bathroom to change my bandage. I removed the old wrap, washed my hand, and took a good look.

Shit.

ADRIAN

The Queen
of the Cats

Fairy tales terrified me when I believed in things. On my fifth
birthday, one of Mama's lady friends, Miss Janice, came over
for dinner. We weren't having a party or anything that year,
just a quiet meal at the kitchen table with huck-a-bucks for
dessert. Miss Janice taught at a university. I remember her as
the kind of lady Mama liked: smart, well educated, not the
type to wear makeup. She was the first black woman I'd ever
seen with short hair. Over dinner, Miss Janice told us about
her travels up and down back roads, through abandoned
farms, into the backwoods and hollers of the South. She'd
been looking for old people to tell her stories, but not just
anyone or any story. Her stories had to be particular.

"All your stories come from one town?" Mama asked.

"That's the thing baby," Miss Janice said, "There's more
than one Okahika."

Before I could open my mouth, Mama pressed her foot into mine. Okahika was where granmè and granddaddy lived. I'd been to Okahika before, plenty of times.

"What are you talking about?" Mama asked.

"Hard to explain," Miss Janice said. "At first, I found all these references to a town called Okahika, but they were in different states: Georgia, Florida, Texas, Arkansas and so on. I found about a dozen, all through the South. But the stories were so similar that they must have come from the same place."

"So is there one Okahika or a bunch?"

"That's what I tried to find out." Miss Janice rested her hand on Mama's. "I drove all over the place looking for people who'd talk about Okahika. Most just repeated stories they'd heard themselves."

A question just popped out of me. "Miss Janice, did you ever find Okahika?"

"Adrian! What have I told you about interrupting grown folk?" Mama snapped.

"I'm sorry," I said.

Miss Janice squeezed Mama's hand and gave me a smile. "Baby, if Okahika ever existed, it's long gone now. But you can read what I found out. Here." Miss Janice handed me a wrapped present. "Althea tells me you're a good reader."

I looked at Mama. She nodded, so I opened the present right at the table. It was Miss Janice's book, *The Mythic Southern: Folktales of Okahika.*

I remember the book more than Miss Janice. It had a yellow and white checkerboard cover with a picture of a red frog on it. My birthday dress was the same color. The stories had crazy titles like "Bell and Cut Mary Somewhere in the Sugarcane," "Immamou," or "Reverend Overtime Gets Himself Together." "The Queen of the Cats" still scares me. Not the ending of that story, but the moment. I'm sure there's a better word for the moment. If I asked Ben, he would mansplain at me, then point me to a book on narrative theory or some bullshit. But I've called it the moment since I was a girl.

The moment is the jump off. It's that one little thing that puts everything else into motion. Little Red Riding Hood takes a basket to her grandmother. The Prince's invitation gets to Cinderella's house. Once the moment happens, the story starts and there's no going back. My problem is that the people in the story never know when the moment happens. By the time they realize the story has started, it's too late. They can look back and say oh *that's* when that happened but by then they're hanging off a cliff. I can handle hanging off a cliff, but not knowing why I'm hanging off a cliff until I'm hanging off just bothers me. If I'm in a story, it's my story. I want to know when it starts.

Miss Janice didn't know how to eat a huck-a-buck, so I showed her how to loosen the Dixie cup from the frozen Kool-Aid and slurp from the bottom. Mama and her friend visited while I finished mine and opened the book. "The Queen of the Cats" jumped off the page and infected me. I never got loose of that story. When Mama tried to read the story to me before bed, I told her I already knew what happened and didn't want to hear it again. She kissed me on the forehead and tucked me in, but I stared at the tin ceiling all night as the story ran across the room, up the walls, and out into the night before it came back and curled itself up under my pillow at sunrise.

A long time ago on a cold night, an elderly nun sat in the warm kitchen of the rectory, waiting for the old priest to come home for dinner after performing funeral rites. Their cat Cady curled up next to the stove, half-asleep and half-waiting for the priest to arrive, in hopes of getting a treat. They waited and waited and waited for hours and began to worry, until at last the priest ran into the rectory, disheveled and dirty, shouting, "Arcadia Forsyth? Who's Arcadia Forsyth?" All the nun and the cat could do was stare and wonder what was the matter.

"Father," the nun said, "What's happened to you? And why are you looking for this Arcadia Forsyth?"

"Mother, you would not believe me if I told you," the priest said. "I can hardly believe it my own self." The priest sank into a kitchen chair and began to shiver. The nun began to bring the priest his dinner, but then thought better of it and poured him a glass of whiskey.

"Here," she said, "warm your bones."

The priest drank the entire glass in one gulp, then refilled his glass. "What a day," he said. "I had just performed the last rites and counseled the family. I left through the back entrance of the cemetery to catch the streetcar. It was already dark and I sat down. I must have been tired, because I fell asleep and only woke when I heard a cat's meow."

"Meow," answered Cady.

"Yes, exactly like that," said the old priest. "So I opened my eyes and guess what I saw?"

"I can't even imagine," the nun said.

"Cats of different types: Siamese, calicos, black cats, and so on. And guess what they carried?"

"Carried?" the nun asked.

The old priest lowered his voice. "A small coffin covered in purple velvet pall, and on the pall was a tiny crown of gold, and at every fourth step they all meowed together."

"Meow," said Cady.

"Yes, exactly like that!" said the old priest. "And as they came closer, I could see them more clearly. You know how cat's eyes reflect the tiniest light. Well they came closer, six carrying the coffin, the seventh walking in front like—well look at Cady staring at me. You'd think she understood me."

"Never mind," said the nun, "What happened next?"

"Well, as I was saying, the seven cats came towards me solemnly, and at every fourth step they said together, 'meow.'"

"Meow," said Cady again.

"Yes, just like that, over and over until they stood at the entrance to the cemetery, right next to me, and then they stopped and stared straight at me. I felt a strangeness inside me, I admit. Now look here at Cady! She's staring at me the way they did."

"Never mind Cady!" the nun said. "Go on."

"Now, this is the part. They stared and I stared back until the seventh cat, the one that wasn't carrying the coffin, said to me, yes, said aloud in a voice, 'Tell Arcadia Forsyth that Arcadio Fearsithe is dead' and that's why I asked you who Arcadia Forsyth was. But how can I tell Arcadia Forsyth that Arcadio Fearsithe is dead if I don't know who Arcadia Forsyth is?"

"Saints preserve us!" screamed the nun. "Cady, look at Cady!"

And to their shock, Cady stared and Cady swelled and at last Cady shrieked, "What? Arcadio is dead? Then I'm the Queen of the Cats!" Cady ran out of the rectory and was never seen again.

While Ben fixed the sink, I tried to fix my hand. It hurt, itched, burned, tingled, tickled, and ached all at once. I used every ointment we had, but nothing in the bathroom relieved my symptoms. I got frantic. I started crying. My hand felt oversized, like all the blood was going in but none could get out. I suppose I had some idea of relieving the pressure, but I honestly couldn't think all the way straight. I don't know why I did what I did. I grabbed a pair of nail scissors, opened them up, and slashed my palm the opposite way, from thumb to pinky, over and over again until a bloody X marked my left palm. The showerhead exploded and rusty-red water splashed into the tub. I felt amazing. Calm, relaxed. Fucking giddy. I giggled again and started laughing, just a little at first, and then louder and louder until I collapsed on the toilet, which shattered into sharp ceramic shards, hurting nothing I cared about.

If Ben understood me, he would leave. My co-workers and clients would run. And this thing, this insect squirming inside me, would have chosen someplace else to hatch. Some place beautiful, full of life and joy and hope and happiness. Not me. I walk, speak, eat when Ben shoves food in my face, fuck when Ben feels like fucking, but that just shows how stupid he is. Only a fool feeds a coffin. Only a fool makes love to a dead woman. Only a fool plants seeds in the desert. Whatever's growing inside me can't live. It had to die, it had to die.

"Adrian!" Ben stood in the doorway. I didn't see him come in. "Holy crap, what happened?"

"It's nothing," I said. "I'm fine."

"The toilet. The shower." His mouth hung open. "You punched a hole in the mirror."

"No I—" I looked up. We'd hung a large framed mirror next to the sink when we moved in so I could see myself before work. The heavy mirror had cracked in the center, creating long, straight lines extending to the edges and shorter connecting lines between the long ones, like a spiderweb cast in glass.

"I didn't," I said as Ben helped me up, "I didn't do that." You have to believe me.

"Let's just get you cleaned up," Ben said. "You've got blood all over your dress."

I looked down. A ragged, bloody X crossed me just below the navel. I didn't remember doing that either.

The bathroom sink still worked. I turned on the water with my right hand and let cool water run over my bloody left. Seemed like a waste with the broken shower running nonstop. Ben kept talking. I didn't pay attention. I stopped enjoying water long ago, but this felt too good, like all the bile inside me got carried off in a flood. I'm not gonna cry. The water felt like every bath before I got dirty, like baptism, like a sudden rain, like a fire hydrant sprinkler on the hottest day of the summer. I felt something else stir inside me, and I let the water carry it off with the rest.

"Oh good," Ben said. How long had I been standing there? A minute, an hour?

"I thought you got cut up pretty bad." He kissed me on the forehead. "Glad you're okay. I'm gonna find the main and turn the water off, and then we can start fixing things."

I was not okay, but when I took my hand out of the water, my palm looked like it always had, slightly red with curving fortuneteller lines. No cuts, no scars. A large cicada flew past my face and landed in the center of the shattered mirror. Then the water shut off, and all the water on the floor drained away through the floorboards until there was nothing left but dust and broken porcelain and blood on my yellow dress.

"Did I get it?" Ben yelled from the lawn.

Yeah, Ben. You got it.

Ben took the car to buy another toilet, mirror, and showerhead. I swept up the broken toilet. I didn't know what else to do. Once I finished sweeping, I wondered if I could take the mirror down without cutting myself again. I wasn't afraid of cutting myself, I was afraid of cutting without consequence. Damaging myself left me a problem I could manage. I caused the pain and I could fix it. But this get-out-of-pain-free card scared the shit out of me. I didn't know who I was without pain.

Whatever broke the mirror left the wooden frame intact. I carefully lifted the mirror off of the wall and carried it to the dining room table. I remembered the mirror being so heavy we had to slide it across the floor, but it lifted easily. The mirror took up the whole surface of the table. Sitting horizontally, the frame blended into the hardwood floor and the spiderweb mirror seemed to float above it, untethered. It drew the eye and held light in a way I'd never seen before. Each piece reflected a different part of me. I looked to one side and saw the hem of my dress. Another facet showed my shoe. I saw my ear sideways, a knee, the back of my neck. I pointed in every direction. I looked to one side and saw cracked sidewalks, a wrought iron fence, filthy floodwater, people laughing on a street corner, a little girl, Marcel on top of me, my mother the moment her water broke, a wooden ship, a broom sweeping, me lying in bed looking at a pressed tin ceiling, a frozen glacier, Free Cookie laying in the sun, a pool of cold water. A flying bird stopped in mid-air, turned its head, and said CHEEPER-CHEEPER TAPE!

I spun around and knocked the mirror off the table. Glass flew across the room. Nothing else moved, nothing else made a sound. I scanned the ceiling and the corners. Nothing. There wasn't any bird in the house.

A chill ran up the entire length of my body. I ran onto the porch. I wiped sweat from my arms and took a few deep breaths. I didn't remember those places or people. I'd never seen a glacier in real life. But some deep part of me had gone there, known those people. No birds in my house.

Adrian, would you like some water with ice?

No, no, I don't belong here. It doesn't matter.

I swept the floors again. I ran my fingers along my palm, looking for something that wasn't there. I looked in the shards of the mirror, wondering if I would see something else. I changed into shorts and an old t-shirt, and sprayed my dress with stain remover. I sat down and did nothing in particular. I wasn't thirsty. I stood up and went to the kitchen. Ben had left the cabinet under the sink open, with all the still-wet contents on the floor. From the looks of it, he'd finished the repair but came to my rescue before the cabinet dried. Kitty litter would soak up all the spilled water. I got the bag of litter and the scoop from the laundry room. I bent down to spread out the litter, and then I had an idea. I placed my hands on the wet cabinet wood. Drain, I thought. Seep, soak, swirl, go away, dry up. Follow your path back into the earth.

Nothing happened. I mean my hands got wet, but nothing else happened. I spread out the kitty litter and put the bag back in the laundry room. Just then, I noticed Free Cookie's food bowl. It was full. It had been full that morning, I knew. I'd filled it. No, I filled it the night before. Had Free Cookie not eaten in a day? In fact, I couldn't remember the last time I'd even seen her. Yesterday? The day before? Maybe the noise scared her off.

"Cookie?" I called.

Cookie didn't answer.

"Cookie?" I called again. Cats don't come when people call them. I poured her food back into the bag, and then refilled it, dropping the food as slowly and loudly as possible. Normally she came running when I filled her food bowl. Nothing.

I looked in all of her favorite napping spots: the porch swing, the living room window, the laundry. She wasn't there. I checked outside. I wish Ben would just let us hire a lawn service. The backyard looked a complete mess of fallen trees branches, tall grass, and overgrown vines. The front yard looked raggedy, but at least he cuts it once in a while. Last year, he planted a peach tree sapling in the front yard. Never grew an inch. I told him that he needed to cut the grass short so the tree would absorb enough nutrients, but he never does. Free Cookie wasn't under the tree, not that it provided enough shade for a cat. I looked around the azaleas and hydrangea bushes, along the line of scrub trees that separates our property from the start of The Through at the end of town, and across our tiny, overgrown back yard. Nothing, nothing, nothing.

"Now ain't she sweet—sweet as a peach—lemme get a look at'cha."

Pats and the Strickland brothers leered at me from the porch of their dilapidated mansion next door. Mending and Wending Strickland grew up in the house Ben and I rent now. Their family built several more houses and most of this end of town. They came into some serious money, everyone knows. What no one says is how they came into money: the old-fashioned land grab. That vacant lot at the end of town, what Ben calls The Through, used to be an all-black town. The Strickland family chased all the residents out, then claimed their land and sold the entire parcel to the railroads. Yet, when my friends and I formed a charitable investment firm, the Stricklands invested right away, and their old money led to new clients.

As a favor, they rent our house to us for next to nothing. At least I thought it was a favor. The house is a small, craftsman-style bungalow with a small porch leading into the living room. We have a fireplace, but it's so old and unsafe we can't use it. Behind the living room is the dining room, and behind that is the kitchen and laundry room. The living room also branches off into a sort of square hallway that leads to our bedroom, Ben's office, and the bathroom. The house is fine. Small, but there's just two of us. The house is not the issue. Pats and the Stricklands are the issue.

When we first moved in, couples rented the lower floor of the Strickland mansion for weddings and anniversary parties. Business tapered off, maybe due to how Mending, pasty white and potbellied, would dress up in an old suit two sizes too small and insist on playing host, while his twin brother Wending, tall and scrawny, ate reception food and drank wine in a pair of dirty boxers and slippers. Their friend, roommate, third wheel, Pats would corner guests and rant about 'them liberals' until his face turned red. Word got around and people stopped booking. Then the trio decided to remodel the place. To make space, they cleaned out antiques, junk, family heirlooms, and just left them on the veranda. A year ago. Remodeling crews came in and out, but they quit coming months ago. The junk's still on the porch, getting mildewy. These days, the three of them sit on the porch getting drunk, especially Pats.

Everyone around here calls him Pats, but no one remembers why. I can't recall anyone ever accusing Pats of having a job, but he always has a bottle of cheap bourbon in a brown paper bag. Every day, he eats breakfast at the cafe up the street by himself, flirts with the waitresses, then ambles down back the to the mansion. In private, women call him Pats the Perv. He hits on every woman he sees, young or old, black or white, single or married. Women come around trying to get people to go to their church and Pats hits on them. Women taking their kids for a walk and Pats hits on them. He's not one of those men who thinks he's God's gift or something. He's sweaty with bad teeth. Pats is just persistent. He's the guy who shows up at a bar just before last call, playing the odds. If he just keeps talking, someone will put something in his mouth to make him stop.

The three of them—Pats, Mending, and Wending—came up right here in Northport, went to school together, ate together, chased girls together, grew old together. They spoke in a duet of three people, each finishing the thought of the other.

"Smile for me—ain't you pretty—come on over."

I smiled and hated myself. "Morning," I said. My body became a disconnected collection of parts under someone else's control. The legs and feet walked past the magnolia that separates their yard from ours. The spine stretched up and forward to push the breasts towards them. The right hand waved, then stuck itself out so the men could paw and kiss its fingers. The feet walked up their stairs and took the body between the men, then froze in place. The eyes saw their dilapidated house and the leer in their grins, the nose smelled cheap bourbon and mildew, the ears heard lust, but none of the senses agreed to share any information, instead locking down, as if each moment in their midst was precious. The thighs and ass felt their thick fingers. The mouth opened into a wide smile and the throat affected a soft, pleasing tone. Only the stomach stayed true to itself, snarling, coiled, furious at them and me.

I am my haint. I haunt my own body.

The men touched my hands, my waist, my cheek, my back. "Ain't seen you lately—just talking about you—sit a spell."

"I wish I could, but I'm looking for my cat."

"Your pussy ran off—gotta be good to the pussy—here pussy, pussy."

The stomach tied hard knots.

"Have you seen her? She's gray, with a white stripe on her face."

"Sounds like some old, wrinkly pussy." They laughed. My left hand balled into a fist, but the right hand, Jezebel, went behind the back and held the left arm above the elbow.

"Well," the mouth said. "I'll check across the street."

Move, feet! Don't just stand there.

"Look at the—hair place they got all kinds of—old pussy up in there."

"Yes well, good talking to you." They touched the body again, here and there. The feet just stood there. A shadow passed over the lawn. The eyes looked up and saw a long prow, a curving hull, a rudder, an old wooden ship, passing over the treetops, trailing a thick rope that fell into the street. The magnolia tree budded and bloomed. A breeze, warm and salty, blew through the tree. Fragrant white petals fell onto the porch, erasing the stink of old men and old bourbon. Cicadas sang. I ran down the steps and across the yard calling, "Hello! Hello!" as if whoever sailed a flying ship would stop and drink sweet tea. I wanted to ask someone if they'd seen it too, but the only other people around were Pats and the Stricklands. I wasn't asking them.

Looking up, the ship sat still while the earth and sky moved past. I ran to the trailing rope and grabbed it. The rope felt rough, but a necessary roughness, as if the rope had work to do and couldn't be bothered to smooth itself out just for me. This was not a rope that would accommodate my needs. I could adapt or let go.

I didn't have any sort of plan. The ship sailed down Main Street and turned left at the river. I held on and followed, listening to the rhythmic wood creaking overhead. Nothing sounds like a wooden ship. I'd never set foot on a sailing ship and I knew it instantly. The ship stopped just before the fence. I closed my eyes and listened. I heard the wheel squeak and the rudder groan in reply. Wind whistled past the mast. Pictures formed in my mind: dark holds beneath the deck, lined with shelves, chains, and manacles, and a large burn mark on the deck. A shudder began on the tip of the mast, ran along the length of the ship, down the rope, and through my left hand.

A cat meowed. I opened my eyes and Free Cookie stood no more than a dozen feet away. "Hey!" I said, but in my surprise, I let go of the rope. The ship bobbed away like a balloon in a parking lot, upwards, upwards, until I could see nothing of her but a tiny dot in a blue sky.

Pablo Picasso's
Les Demoiselles d'Avignon

In 1906, Henri Matisse showed his friend and rival, Pablo Picasso, a mask from the Dan/Gio People of West Africa. Then in May or June of 1907, the Musée du Trocadéro introduced Parisian audiences to African masks and carvings. The Trocadéro exhibits deeply influenced Picasso, and later inspired the poet-philosopher Léopold Sénghor.

In the early 20th century, Westerners saw Africa antithetically, as not-Europe, a dark, disordered and primitive place ruled by superstition. The museum codified this common sentiment by lowering the lights, and placing the artifacts into a carefully constructed jumble, with some objects laying on the floor, others obscured or facing away from the viewer. In traditionally pantheistic West African cultures, masks, when worn by a consecrated dancer, became avatars of certain gods or spiritual forces. When not in use, masks were kept isolated in their own houses of worship. One spiritual visitor might deliver an important message; multiple visitors either foretold or caused a calamity. Thus, these authentic ritual objects were never meant to occupy the same space at the same time.

Picasso attended the Trocadéro exhibition. While there, he reportedly encountered an overwhelming smell of "rot" and a desire to run from the room. Did Picasso smell something physically rotting, or was he unable to comprehend African images without some sense of disgust and panic? Were other forces at work? This is what we know for sure: instead of leaving, the young painter stayed and studied the art for hours.

Later, he told a friend, "Men had made those masks and other objects for a sacred purpose, a magic purpose, as a kind of mediation between themselves and the unknown hostile forces that surround them, in order to overcome their fear and horror by giving it a form and an image. At that moment I realized that this was what painting was all about. Painting isn't an aesthetic operation; it's a form of magic designed as a mediator between this strange, hostile world and us, a way of seizing the power by giving form to our terrors as well as our desires." In this moment, Picasso discovered a new purpose for painting, which eventually lead him to depict all sides of an object at once, now known as Cubism. However, Picasso failed to grapple with the limits of his own worldview, largely drawn from Modernist writers and artists who frequented Café Els Quatre Gats.

In any case, Picasso's revelation influenced the style in which he painted *Les Demoiselles d'Avignon*, especially in the treatment of the two figures on the right side of the composition. While often seen as two separate women, they can also be seen as spiritual representations, or "all sides" of the three figures on the left. Although *Les Demoiselles* is seen as a proto-cubist work, Picasso developed a style derived from African art before beginning the Analytic Cubism phase of his painting in 1910. Other works of Picasso's African Period (1906-1909, also known as the Negro Period) include *Bust of a Woman*, *Mother and Child*, *Nude with Raised Arms*, and of course, *Three Women*.

Picasso and Me

One day – I was maybe 8 or so – my mother took me aside and said, "Ben, you'll never be handsome or a good dancer. So you need to be smart and get a good job. That's the only way you'll attract a woman." I'm sure she meant it for the best. Don't mothers mean things for the best? I'm sure she meant it for the best. But 'you'll never be handsome' stuck with me in all the wrong ways. I never embraced it. I just tried to prove her wrong. Maybe that's where my life went off-course, so to speak. No direction. Running from, not towards. Swept off by a deep, subterranean current, powerful, swift, born in the days of dinosaurs, nor caring if I go this way or that, as long as I go. Maybe that's the center of my personal whirlpool. I should be much farther downstream, metaphorically speaking, almost out to sea, past all the places on the map, out where it says Here Be Dragons.

And yet here I am, still going in circles.

I don't remember where we were at the time. Me and Mom. Isn't that odd? I should remember.

And yet here I am, still going in circles.

After I work half the night installing a new toilet, I take a morning jog past the old railroad trestle along the Black Warrior River. I'm not much of a jogger – flat feet – but supposedly even 30 minutes of activity lowers blood pressure and prevents dementia so any little bit helps. I pull up a podcast on my phone while I jog, never music, always something educational, boring, yes boring, but the story keeps me going. I don't know why I'm like that. Hardheaded—even when I know I'm wrong.

The jogging path takes 1.6 miles from start to finish. Two laps equal a 5K. I'm keeping a good pace today. One-two, one-two. I'm on pace to end my run with the end of the podcast.

A woman waves at me. I want to ignore her. Keep going, I tell myself. Just let her pass. Do not engage. She waves again. This is so awkward. How am I supposed to respond? A wave? A wave and a hello. Just say hello. But I'm almost home. I've passed the bakery at the corner that makes all the wedding cakes, where the jogging path melds into the sidewalk of the little tourist-trap-town I inhabit. Wealthy people come to eat gourmet pork rinds in paper bags, or pose for pictures in front of Northport Willy's Old-Timey Barber Shop, or the Downtown Five and Dime, or Mrs. Potts Emporium and General Store, or my house, or the place next door, or any spot that fulfills the Southern fantasy. Some nights, the good

old boys drive drunk up and down the street in their huge
4x4 pickup trucks, waving Confederate flags and screaming. I
want to call the cops on those nights, but I don't.

I'm right at the bakery when I realize the woman turned
around and followed me. Now she's right behind me.

"Yo," she says. "Ho-tep!"

I relax. My name's not Hotep.

"Talking to you, Hotep," she says.

"Are you talking to me?"

"How many Hotep niggas you see?"

I want to look around but I don't. Instead, I look squarely
at this woman. She's black, dark, sweating. Her hair hangs
limp around her neck. She looks like she runs well, like maybe
she was on the track team in high school, but it's been a decade
since she really trained. Her belly bulges slightly under her teal
sports bra. Her pink sneakers turned black around the toes.
I shouldn't judge. I'm no prize either. I played football and
lacrosse in high school, but running always kept me going.
Now I'm older and slower, wearing an old pair of khaki shorts
and a plain gray t-shirt. She looks at me looking at her and I
feel the sudden need to vanish.

"We need to talk," she says and grabs my wrist. Her hands
feel cool, almost cold.

"Talk about what?" I ask. I confess: I'm bad with faces. I
almost drowned jumping into a friend's pool on a dare when
I was 8. I didn't know how to swim. His parents rescued me,
but I'd already lost too much oxygen. I can't always connect

faces with names or names with voices. Maybe I know this woman. Could be. When I meet people, I have to play along until I get some clue. Otherwise, I'm just lost.

"Better recognize, Hotep."

I have no idea who this woman is, or why she's calling me Hotep. Nothing in her posture or voice gives any clue. Her voice though, her voice sings out. She wants something personal.

"Can I help you with something?"

"I don't give a fuck," she says.

"What?"

"I. Don't. Give. A. Fuck," she repeats, and then adds, "You need to get up off your ass."

"I need?"

"To get up. Off your ass," she says.

I can almost see my house from here. My cat is probably patrolling the backyard, happy since I haven't mowed in weeks. Free Cookie, the cat I found in front of the Free Cookie sign, believes she is a dangerous and deranged killer stalking hapless prey through the underbrush. I can't disturb her fantasy.

"I'm not sure we've met."

"You don't know me? The fuck you saying? You don't know me?"

A little whine creeps into my voice. I hate that. "I need to finish up my run and go home," I say.

"Jogging is for the suburban bourgeoisie." She looks me up and down. "You can do better."

"I don't live in the suburbs. How I stay healthy is none of your business."

"Whatever's clever, Hotep."

"Why are you calling me that?"

"Whatever."

"Are you with Amway or something?"

"Amway?" she scoffs. "Your broke ass can't afford no Amway. You an adjunct English professor with no savings and a secret job grading AP exams on the DL. If your Chair ever finds out, you're fired. But you want to quit anyway. So maybe I should go down to the office and tell him that Professor Hotep want to quit his damn job."

"How—who are you?"

"Quiet as it's kept, Ben Hotep. Believe that."

And she walks back the way she came without another word.

The podcast has been playing in my earphones the entire time. The NYU professor has moved to the Q&A portion. No one thinks to put the questions on a microphone so she gives disembodied answers that don't make much sense. On the street, an enormous man with a white beard straddles his enormous motorcycle and sits heavily. Next to him, little metal posts topped with horseheads line the curb, spaced about 3 feet apart. Metal rings run through the horses' teeth. Perhaps the artist intended for the metal horseheads to bite the rings like real horses, but budget cuts. Someone just drilled holes through their metal teeth and stuck a ring through. I suppose people tied up their horses to these horseheads back in the old days. Or the city just put those in to make us look more old-timey and get tourists.

My legs have gone cold. I finish the run from sheer stubbornness knowing I'll pay later. Like that character in the old Popeye cartoons. What was his name? I'll gladly pay you Tuesday for a hamburger today.

I sit heavily on my front porch. My legs shake.

Quiet as its kept, Ben Hotep. Believe that.

What the hell did she mean? The Chair doesn't care who else I teach for, as long as the students don't complain and I turn in my grades on time. I doubt he even knows my name. I can't remember any woman talking to me like that before. An ex? Did I date someone who talks like that? She called me Hotep. People used that nickname in college, 20 years ago. More. It can't mean the same thing now. Like Hawthorne's scarlet letter embroidered and reworked until it turns into the logo of The University of Alabama, names and symbols change over time. That's one of my best lectures.

'Ben', I meant to say. 'My name is Professor Ben Hughes. Have we met? Perhaps at a party? Or did we *meet* at a party?' I used to party hard back in the day. Before I met my girlfriend. But why would an ex or a girl I met at some party – I don't even go to those kinds of parties anymore – track me down and start talking gibberish? That makes no sense at all.

Free Cookie curls herself around my shins, leaving me covered in fine gray hair.

"Cookie, what do you think?"

Free Cookie doesn't answer.

Look, I say to myself, I'm not responsible for her feelings about anything. I can't control her actions. Maybe I do know her. Maybe we hooked up once at a party long ago and she developed feelings. When was the last time I went to a party and hooked up with someone? Years ago. Many years ago. And it only happened once and this wasn't her. So strike that. But whoever she is, she has feelings that have nothing to do with my current situation. I'm in a relationship and I have a job. I can't fix her problems. She needs a therapist. She needs a good therapist. I need to concentrate on finishing my manuscript so I can get published and apply for tenure-track jobs. Once I land something, I can pay off my student loans, buy a house, and get on with my life. Maybe I'll ask Adrian to marry me.

I go inside, turn the TV on, and pick an old sci-fi show to watch while I cool-down stretch. A black space captain in the 24th century goes back in time to the 1950s and believes he's a sci-fi author writing about a black space captain in the 24th century.

Quiet as it's kept, Ben Hotep.

Suburban bourgeoisie.

Who says bourgeoisie out loud?

As a matter of fact, she acted like I knew who she was the whole time. Like we had a relationship. An ongoing thing I knew about. Like she puts something in and I put something in and we both get something back. Like Picasso seeing an

African mask for the first time, which revolutionized his work but also led to the raiding and exploitation of West African artifacts throughout the 20th century.

That didn't really work out for one side.

I know, in relationships, which side is Picasso and which side is me.

And now the captain has a breakdown and gets thrown in an asylum and starts writing on walls but nothing makes sense because I've been thinking about her instead of paying attention.

I stop the show and get up, slowly. My legs cramp up. I'm dehydrated. I didn't drink water after today's run. As I walk to the kitchen, my phone rings. I should let it go to voicemail, which I will never, ever check. But this could be a job, or a publication, or something big. Or her. A woman who could track me down on the street probably has my phone number. I sigh and look around the living room. Here's what I'll say: Hello strange woman in the sports bra. I'm so glad you called again. I know we shared something once. Your feelings for me are intense. But I don't think I can listen to your feelings and participate in your healing at the same time. Right. I can be your friend or your therapist but not both. So I think you should find someone – a professional – who you can talk to. I'll support – you will? Great. Talk to you later.

It's 11:39 am. Adrian is video calling. "Hey!" she says. She looks amazing and crisp, even in the human broiler that is late summer Alabama. That amazing hair, wild and naturally kinky. Deep-brown skin. That wide mouth that leaves me speechless when she smiles. She doesn't smile much anymore, but I watch the crinkles around her lips, her dimple, little signs that she might smile today. She wore a flowered sundress to work, only because she's not meeting any clients. The dress looks fine on video, but nothing compares to the real thing.

"Hey," I say.

"How are you? What are you doing? You look beat."

"Just stretching after my run."

"Good run today?" Adrian asks.

"Sure, sure" I say. Adrian rubs her hands under her desk. "Any reason for a call? You usually text."

"Well," she leans in, "I wondered if you heard anything about a job."

"Nothing yet," I say. I always have to say that.

"Well, I heard of a lead," she says.

"Okay."

"Can you do line editing?"

"Line editing?"

"Someone I know works for a company," a co-worker hands Adrian a manila folder, "that works with writers. They're looking for someone to fix up," Adrian leafs through the folder, "submissions they're ready to publish. Essays, academic articles, stuff like that. APA style guide stuff. The job is part-time—at first—but if things go well..."

"Whoa," I say. "Hold up. APA style? I don't know APA style."

"I thought you taught APA in your composition classes."

"Well yeah, but I never actually check to see if they're doing it right."

"How do you grade them?"

"I'm a novelist." Who's never published a novel. "I just make it up as I go. Besides, I'd prefer a tenure-track job at a smallish liberal arts college."

"Didn't you used to tutor in the university writing center?"

"That doesn't count."

"Yeah, it counts." She's getting exasperated with me. I can tell by the way she exhales on the 'ow' in counts. Her shoulders slump and she looks up.

"Seriously, I have no idea what I'm talking about. I just look in the style guide and tell them to do it like that. I never check to see whether or not they actually do it."

"It doesn't have to be perfect, I'm sure. Just close enough to submit to whatever."

"I can't do close enough," I snap.

"Fine," she says.

No one says anything.

"Soooo the tenure-track thing," Adrian says. "Do you have any interviews?"

"Well, my sources tell me that I'm in the running for several positions. Once the committees make their shortlists, I'll know one way or another." My sources consist of other adjuncts trying for the same jobs, and a Wiki page dedicated to adjuncts complaining about the adjuncts that got the jobs. "If I don't get an interview, I'll consider the APA gig."

"You will? Okay. What's today's date? Do you know?"

I had to think about it. "August 27th," I say. "No, it's the 28th."

"Okay great. There's a program coming on the radio later. Can you record it for me?"

"Sure, of course," I say. "I can download it for you. What's the show?"

"It's about those bugs that make noise all night."

"Cicadas?"

"Right. Did you know they run on cycles? Like once a decade. An expert is going to talk about the Alabama cycle."

"Really? Okay, sure. Why are you even interested?"

"I might use their cycle in a pitch." Adrian moved in with me a few years ago and almost immediately entered grad school. After she graduated, Adrian and some MBA friends formed a firm telling rich people that it's okay to be rich. Adrian makes more money than I ever will.

"That's a good idea."

Adrian changes gear. "You know, you could, you know, not look for work."

"My contract runs through the end of next semester. After that," I admit, "I've got nothing lined up."

"That's my point. Look, I can cover our bills."

"What would I be? Your houseboy?"

"Ow!" Adrian says. She shakes her hand like she's throwing water off her fingertips.

"What's wrong?" I ask.

"It's nothing. Paper cut. Hey, I'll get you some short-shorts," she teases. "Just think about it."

"Okay."

"Okay?"

With every bit of manliness I had left, I said, "I'll think about it."

"Ok good," she said. "By the way, have you seen Cookie?"

"Cookie?" I asked. "Sure, she's right—" I step outside and look behind the wilting hydrangea. "She was right there a minute ago."

"Well can you look around for her? She's been missing for days."

"Missing?"

"We talked about it last night. I thought I saw her after you left, but I was wrong. She hasn't touched her food."

"In days."

"So can you look for her?" Her shoulders slump again.

"Sure. Of course, sure," I say. "I'll go find Cookie."

"Check under the railroad trestle behind the house. And the other way, down close to the river, around the pilings. I've seen other cats around there. You know where I'm talking about?"

"Pilings?"

"That's what they're called, right? Those huge concrete things that hold the bridge up? Right by the river where the kids cut through the fence? There's an old dock there. We've walked past it a million times."

When I first became an adjunct English professor, I half-thought that the job came with a used Subaru Outback, one of those tweed jackets with the elbow patches, and automatic NPR membership. The Gore 2000 bumper sticker might cost extra. But instead I got absent-minded. I became the absent-minded adjunct. Maybe it's how I deal with the stress of a dead-end job. I just don't think about it, or I forget this and that, or maybe I just don't care anymore. But I miss things Adrian has an eye for. Architecture. Types of trees. Places cats hang out. We can go out for a walk and she'll see everything while I'm asking myself if I'm a failure because so-and-so from grad school has a book out with Tiny Hardcore Press and a review in the LA Times and a magazine spread in GQ and I don't. I haven't finished a new story in years.

"Are you there?"

"Yes, yes," I say. "Pilings. Cicadas. Got it."

"Thanks honey, gotta go," she says and hangs up.

I sit there. I put the phone down.

How would Adrian get down to the river? I'm not sure when she'd have time to go. To get down there, she'd have to climb over a chain-link fence. The Black Warrior River is deep. People drown all the time, so why would she even go down there in the first place? What client cares about cicadas?

I turn NPR on.

NPR runs a feature on someone's new book.

I turn NPR off.

After a few minutes, I check the local NPR affiliate website and find a link for the show. "Cicadas: The Clock of the World, a new book by..." Great. I just missed the exact thing Adrian wanted me to hear. They typically post the podcast version a few hours after the on-air show. I need to redeem myself. I look behind the hydrangea again. Cookie's still not there. Maybe I just imagined our cat curling around my legs. Sunlight beams down into our small front yard. People here really show off their lawn skills, but ours isn't much. I planted a little peach tree last year to absorb the sunlight before it heats up the house. So far, it hasn't grown an inch. I've tried mulching, fertilizer, everything. The tree came with a one-year warranty. Adrian wants me to dig it up and take it back. Maybe I should.

Cicadas whirr and chirp in the trees, sounding like the inner workings of a clock so massive we don't realize we're inside it. I've never seen a cicada. I have no idea what they look like. Like grasshoppers I suppose. We hear them so often it's easy to forget they exist. They become background noise, like the trains that still lumber across the river trestle with loads of Alabama coal.

The cicadas make so much noise that everything else on the street drowns under a blanket of clockwork sounds. Young black women in loose gray uniforms push old ladies in wheelchairs to the hair salon across the street. A man rides a lawnmower. Magnolia buds fall from trees. A car passes slowly, turns around, and drives back the way it came. A shirtless man, sweating, jogging, pushes an infant in an expensive stroller. Squirrels eat fallen pecans. While I watch this world under the clockwork cicadas, I think, I just saw that cat, she was just here, Free Cookie was just here, I saw her, I don't need to look for her, why do I have to look, there's fur on my legs. I'm not a cat person. Finding her under that sign was just a fluke, really. Wrong place, wrong time. I walked up and Free Cookie jumped into my arms, just like that. I took her home and my girlfriend thought I'd gone to all this trouble to rescue an orphaned cat.

"How can people abandon cats like that," she asked. "You're so wonderful," she said, and she kissed me like she used to kiss me when we first dated. I never told her I really had nothing to do with it. And then the hero bit wore off and we went back to normal. So what now? What if I find Free Cookie? What will I do? What am I supposed to use, harsh language?

Cookie, go home. Dammit.

Not so long ago, I was the wunderkind. Smart, ambitious, experimental. I was going to change everything with my books. In high school, I read Dad's old Black Revolutionary books: *Soul on Ice, The Autobiography of Malcolm X, The Wretched of the Earth* – and decided I would lead the next revolution. And then college came and there was a student-led revolt on campus, but I didn't lead it. I tell people I was part of the big shutdown, the day when the students occupied the President's office until he divested from apartheid-supporting companies.

I tell people that I sat in the hallway outside his office, risking expulsion, arrest, even death. I didn't. I chickened out. A fight broke out, but the cops had nothing to do with it. Protestors fought each other and I decided that the revolution would best be served by me going to class. Just like that. Maybe that's where I went wrong. Maybe I missed the one little thing everyone else figured out. All talk and hype, but no substance to back it up. Just bobbing along. What's wrong with me? What is wrong with my life? How did I go from aspiring revolutionary to broken down adjunct English professor who makes so little that his girlfriend thinks they'd be better off if he did nothing? What's so wrong with letting a cat hang out under a bridge? It's not like she's going to jump into the river. She's happy with her life. Other people seem happy with their lives. They go to work, come home, watch movies, and they're happy, content, fulfilled. I walk through door and can't remember why I'm there, so I go back and can't figure out why I went back. I'm 45 years old and here I am, grading freshman papers, watching TV, looking for cats.

B E N

A Disheveled Dryad Loveliness

An hour after Adrian calls, I pause next to the fence at the entrance of The Through. I don't know if The Through is the right name for this place. The Through sounds planned, but it doesn't look planned at all. The Through looks like leftover construction pits, letter-of-the-law repairs, erosion gullies, mud ruts from kids parking their trucks to make out, all weaving around the concrete pillars that support an old railroad bridge. A Through, strictly speaking, has a way in and a way out, and goes from one place to another in a more or less straight line. *The* Through starts near my house, meanders under the bridge for maybe the length of a football field, spreads out left and right, and ends when it ends. A chain link fence covered in flowering vines separates The Through from the river.

I walk around abandoned cars, old trees, and the occasional scrappy bush. If anyone had planned, The Through would be as wide as the bridge, some twenty feet across, but it widens and shrinks at will. I can't even say it begins by my house either, that's just where I find it. And as I walk towards the fence, I realize no one ever taught me that this area was called The Through. The neighbors didn't come to me when I moved and say, 'Hey, see that area under the bridge, where the stray cats hang out? That's called The Through. Remember those words: The Through.' That never happened. But we all call it The Through anyway.

From what I've heard – according to the elder of the two Strickland brothers (who grew up in my house but always coveted the larger and grander house next door, bought the larger house when the original owners came on hard times, then converted it into a bed-and-breakfast that failed, where they now sit on the porch eating boiled peanuts and talking at people), a poor black neighborhood once ran from my house down to the river. No paved roads or signs, just a collection of ramshackle houses on cheap land. The Through used to be the main street for this part of town. Their house (my house) survived a flood that wiped out everyone in the black part of town. Everything turned to mud. Former homes got torn down, or declared unfit for children and then torn down. Eventually the city took the land by eminent domain, and then sold it to the railroads. They bulldozed whatever was left and built a bridge over it. The Through faded until only old people could use it for directions. 'Go to The Through and take a left, past the stack of old tires, under the trestle bridge, bear right, and you'll get where the Tastee-Freez used to be,' that sort of thing. On hot days when the air is just right in The Through, I see shimmers of homes, gardens, children doing chores, laughing women with hips leaned over low fences. Today though, I only see immense spiderwebs blowing in a tiny breeze.

Why would Adrian ever go here? She hates mud, ever since Katrina. We can't talk about Katrina. It's like Fight Club: the first rule of Katrina is you don't talk about Katrina. I'm not sure what happened to her. She never talks about it. If NPR refers to Katrina or New Orleans at all, she'll walk out of the room. She never calls anyone from New Orleans and no one calls her, not even her mother. She must have other family, but we've never heard from them. Maybe her mother died, or the family died, or the family thinks Adrian died and there's a grave for her somewhere. When I try to figure it out, my head swells like an overinflated balloon. I mean, it feels overinflated. I don't think my head actually changes shape.

Note to self: check your head.

Sunlight cuts through the branches. Shadows slide over my shirt and shorts as I pass under the trestle, then break into kaleidoscopic patterns on the ground. Even when the wind picks up again, the shadows stick to the ground like tattoos inked in a foreign language.

All is still. Quiet. I can almost hear feral cats sleeping. A few small clouds fly overhead, bright white, so large and fluffy they resemble an old Monty Python skit. I sway, as if I'd stepped onto a moving ship. It's getting hot.

I'm still in my jogging clothes: old cargo shorts, gray t-shirt, blue sneakers. Sweat drips off my forehead. I'm allergic to perfumes and laundry dyes, so I wash my clothes with unscented, dye-less detergent. Yet I smell something coming from my shirt. A musty odor like mildew but stronger, like mildew grew in my nose.

I look under every piece of junk and every bush. What's the advice? When injured, dogs go far, cats go low.

"Free Cookie?" Brush and old tires swallow my voice.

I pause next to the opening in the fence Adrian mentioned. I should check the other side, but I don't want to. I mean I do, but I don't. I don't know what I'm thinking, of course I should go.

A man named Randolph hangs around this end of town. He walks up and down Main Street every day, usually in the mornings. I've seen him wandering around The Through several times. He's here now. Randolph is tall and spare, lean, brown from birth and years outdoors, with perpetually bloodshot eyes. Randolph isn't much for words, but we chat from time to time. He sees me. I wave. He doesn't wave back.

"Randolph, hey!"

Randolph mumbles a few words that might have been a greeting. I know from prior experience that he will not repeat himself if I ask.

"Hot day huh?"

Randolph says nothing, but he stops next to me. His body speaks for him: dirt under his fingernails, sweat on his forehead, and the sense that he's moving even when he stands still.

"The city should do something about this place," I say, but The Through swallows my voice. "The city should do something about this place. Or the neighborhood association could organize a cleanup day."

Randolph's eyes narrow. He turns around and points his long fingers at an old tire near the end of the road.

"There", Randolph says, "My granddaddy place. My mama all her folk born. Barber shop," he says, "and and general store." Randolph points past the fence. "Cow and chicken graze up over. My wife people house over. Church-house hold school five day a week. Baptism in the water. Sweetest peaches you ever grow on this earth right next."

As he speaks, I see little shimmers again. The fence vanishes while houses and shops appear. Next to the old tires, a man fixes his car while friends sip coffee and offer advice. An elderly woman plants saplings where broken stumps stand now. Discarded lumber stands up and forms a fence, a store, a school. People greet each other. Children play chase. An old man in a neat shirt and suspenders leans against a post, watching pretty girls go by while his wife takes a pie out of the oven. I inhale and can't stop. The smell of cinnamon and sweet potatoes fills me and my body expands like an overfed melon. I float away. I'm still inhaling. I'm going to burst. I look down and see myself seeing a town that isn't there and

I can't reconcile the two. I'm still inhaling. Either I'm up here or down there and suddenly, just like that, I'm back to normal size next to the hole in the fence looking at Randolph, breathing in and out, in and out.

"What—" I start.

"Okahika," Randolph declares.

"What?"

"Oh-kah-hee-kah," Randolph pronounces slowly. "Home."

Randolph walks through the hole in the fence and heads right, upriver. I watch him until he disappears behind some overgrown bushes. I look back at the entrance. No digging dog or kid smoking weed made this hole. Someone neatly cut the chain-link in a more or less rectangular shape, maybe four feet high by about two feet wide, but left the razor wire atop the fence intact. Green vines with bright yellow and orange flowers cover most of fence in both directions. I can see the other side, but Free Cookie could hide under a bush or behind a tree. I have to go in. I can slip through easily, but so can anyone else.

A yellow sign says NO ENTRANCE. What if I'm caught on the wrong side and get arrested? The neighborhood association would love that. Randolph would love that. Mending and Wending Strickland would cackle and throw peanuts, and their buddy would say that's what you get for renting to the nigras. So I can't go.

I'll tell Adrian, 'Look, I went down there but a sign said No Entrance.'

She'll say, 'Hey, don't worry. I'm sure it's fine.'

Then I'll say, 'Don't be like that.'

And she'll say, 'I'm not being like anything.'

And I'll apologize or start a fight I can't win. Either way, I'll wind up right back here looking at a hole in a fence.

A few cicadas rattle softly in the bushes. I hear each insect distinctly. One sings, another answers in a different rhythm. At night, they sing as a chorus, but in the daytime, each cicada sings to its special someone. Not to me. I'm no one's special someone.

I turn NPR on. Adrian's program started while I procrastinated. Shit. I fumble around with my phone to get it to record and play at the same time and miss everything but the last seconds. "...as suddenly as it began, suddenly ceases."

"Thank you," the announcer says. "Jean Fontana's new book, *Cicadas: The Clock of the World*, will be on sale tonight after his lecture. 7 pm, in Smith Hall on the University campus. Free and open to the public. Next up, local humorist Michael Martone reads from his new memoir, *Four Four Four Four*."

I turn NPR off.

I'll have to download the program when I get home. I don't know how Adrian can turn cicadas into a client pitch. Then again, she makes the money, and I make dinner. I look around again. Everything stays the same. Trees are trees, junk is junk, and a hole in a fence is just a hole in a fence. I walk through.

Beyond the fence, there's not much to see. An old, white, plastic chair with no back legs leans on the bare ground. Some tall bush with iridescent red berries grows overhead. Weeds. An old rope. Just the sort of hunting ground Free Cookie would like, but nothing cat-shaped makes an appearance. I hear the high-pitched squeaking of bats roosting in the girders that carry the coal bridge. A white and gray pigeon with iridescent green feathers on its chest lands in front of me, walks about bobbing its head for a few seconds, then takes off. Its shadow grows as the bird ascends past the red berries and over the river, growing fainter until I can't see any difference between the shadow and the river. I just stand there for a second. I'm sure it's longer than a second, but I'm not sure how long. Or maybe somewhere, some mechanism deep inside my brain counts the number of heartbeats I forfeit standing there staring at nothing and checks them off my tally, or my inner ear detects minute changes to the gravitational pull of the earth on my body as we hurtle around the sun, which is itself circling the center of our galaxy, moving further and further from the place of its birth to parts unknown. But all I'm really doing is staring at the shadow of a bird passing over water.

Gradually, I become aware of something – someone. Someone is there. She's saying something. To me. She's saying something to me.

"Where you at Hotep?"

I turn around but no one's there.

"Yo, Hotep."

I turn around again and she's right in front me. How did that happen?

"Hotep, you with me?"

She's the jogger from this morning. I mean, she has to be. No one else calls me Hotep, not anymore. But she's older than I remember. She looks like one of the church ladies my mother plays cards with. Sixty-ish, small, trim, wearing pink yoga shorts and a Lycra shirt. I can't see through her shirt. Maybe I didn't get a good look this morning, or maybe this is someone else. Her chest heaves like she just stopped running, and her dark gray hair sticks to her skull. Her abs look fantastic, and her hips move easily. She'd be great in bed.

"Hello, Hotep?"

Note to self: find out what Hotep means these days.

"Um, yes," I say. "I mean, hello."

"Got a smoke?"

"Quit, sorry."

"Aight," she says. "Shouldn't smoke no way." The woman leans over, slowly stretching her lower back. She spreads her feet just past the shoulders, bends over until her hair touches the ground, revealing a slender neck covered in fine gray fuzz. She entwines her arms behind her back and lifts her wrists. I can feel her muscles straining, stretching, just from looking at her. Then she gives a little jerk and pops her spine. She unbends herself slowly until I see myself in her sunglasses again.

"Live round here?" the woman asks.

"Yeah," I reply, and look vaguely back the way I came, except that I can't see my house anymore. Past the old car, and the place where the store used to – it doesn't really matter. I just point back.

"What bring you down this way?"

"I'm looking for my cat. I saw her this morning, but my girlfriend says she's been missing for days." Sweat runs down my arms. I should have brought water with me. "She says she saw the cat over here."

"What kinda cat?"

"Grey-and-white, with a stripe down her face. Notch in one ear but I don't remember which."

"Name?"

"Name?"

"Your cat got a name?" she asks, narrowing her eyes at me behind her sunglasses. At least that's what I think she's doing.

"Free Cookie," I reply.

"Like the sign?" she asks.

"Yes." I say. "That's where I found her."

"You name your cat after a sign?"

"I suppose I did," I admit.

"A motherfucking sign?"

I nod.

"No imagination," she says. She takes off her sunglasses and seems to relax. Now I can see she's older than I thought at first, something about the way her skin stretches across her forehead, or the crinkles by her eyes. Her lopsided upper lip curves like a woman's silhouette.

"Gray-and-white cat, stripe down her face, huh?" the older woman says. "Gray-and-white cat, stripe down her face. Big cat?"

"Not really," I say.

The older woman thinks for a few seconds, then twists her spine so her hips face me, but her face looks almost backwards, towards an old bench. She unravels and then twists the other way.

"Damn! That's better. I get stiff now. I get so stiff now."

I mumble something about muscles.

"Yeah, saw that cat," she says. "Didn't see no notch, but she grey-and-white, stripe on the face."

"When did you see her?"

"Baby, that's a good question. Every day look the same. Every day look the same. Maybe I notice that cat round three or four days ago. All the cats hang out down here. Some live down here, some live in the neighborhood. Eventually, all the cats hang out down here."

A bird I've heard before cries, CHEEPER-CHEEPER TAPE! CHEEPER-CHEEPER-CHEEPER TAPE!

"Thanks for the tip," I say. I want to ask her why she repeats herself so much, and why she calls me Hotep, and if she called me Hotep this morning and miraculously aged 30 years since then. Or if there's a Hotep sign on my back that no one told me about.

"Set a while, Hotep," she says, "All the cats come by here. And besides, if you keep snooping someone a call the cops and get you shot."

"I can't just wait for my cat to show up."

"When someone knocks, answer the door. Just set with me. I'll stretch out my stiffness and you watch. We both watch. Two eyes are better than none. Talk to me."

I look at my watch. 2:36. I still need to make dinner, dry the laundry, and download Adrian's show, but those won't take long.

"Well, okay. Ttwenty minutes," I say.

She walks towards a small hill and I follow, stepping lightly across the scrubby grass. She limps, her right leg taking more weight than her left. She stops and motions for me to walk next to her.

"Gotta replace that hip," she says. "Getting old Hotep, getting old."

We climb the small hill and reach an iron and wood bench facing the entrance, with a red cooler underneath the seat. The cooler seems odd, but no odder than the bench or the rest of my day. Cigarette butts, condom wrappers, and melted Coke bottles litter the ground. A green and white dollhouse sits on a low pole, but when I look closer I see it's a small library with magazines and paperbacks. The old woman takes her phone from her pocket and switches on some music. Given her age, I expected gospel or Motown. Instead, she plays wild jazz music, dissonant and harmonious all at once. A trumpet and saxophone play a duet, but not the same song. It's like listening to two people talk on two different phones to two other people. It's unlike anything I've ever heard.

"Albert Ayler," she says. "1966."

"Never heard of him," I reply.

"Lots you ain't heard, Hotep," she says. "Set down. Set with me."

From the top of the hill, I can see over the fence and through The Through, every pillar, broken bottle, and dumped car all the way back past the train trestle. I can even see the end of Main Avenue, where everything got wiped out, and the edge of my house. If she was standing here before, she could have been watching me the whole time.

Behind us, a long slope leads to the Black Warrior River. There's more room here than I imagined. Thick grass sweeps down the bank, dotted with pink wildflowers. Upriver, I can see the last concrete pilings before the bridge crosses the river. Downriver, I can see more grass, occasionally eclipsed by ornamental plants, remnants of some long-forgotten beautification program. Disheveled dryad loveliness. I read that phrase in a book once and it always stuck with me. Despite the trash and weeds, The Through and the riverbank still maintain a disheveled dryad loveliness. No, this place looks like an underwater garden gone dry. Not a place for a dryad. What's the water equivalent? I should know this. Naiad? Mermaid? Undine? Despite the trash and the weeds, The Through and the riverbank maintain an ungainly undine loveliness. That's not right either.

"I used to do landscaping in college," I say.

"Uh-huh," the older woman says.

"A buddy had a landscaping business. I was grunt labor mostly. Kept me in great shape."

"Sure it do."

"I'd love to have a yard like this."

"Ain't no yard," she says.

"Nothing like this." I point to the long sweep of grass leading to the river. "Just a little plot in front of my house, very flat. A hydrangea and a little peach tree that won't grow. That's it," I say. "You sit alone here all the time?"

"I do. You don't."

I realize I'm still standing. I sit down. "You sit here a lot?" I ask.

"Time to time. I run along the river, stop here, catch my breath, keep moving. Sometime I take a break, but I mostly keep going. Want a beer?" She pats the red cooler. "Got beer."

"No, I'm fine," I say, even though I want a drink.

"Ain't no thing."

"Thanks, I'm good," I say. "Shouldn't you be—I don't know?"

"Praying? Looking at pictures of my grandkids?"

"Something like that."

She snorts. "Ain't got time for some old lady bullshit. Why ain't you work? Ain't got no job? Why ain't you work?"

"Not really," I admit.

"Unemployed?"

"I quit. I'm quitting. I will quit."

"Landscaping?" she asks.

"No," I reply. "I'm a college professor. Adjunct. I teach classes, grade papers, keep students happy."

"You quit?"

"I've got a semester left. After that, I'm not going back."

"What for?"

I don't have a good answer, so I just look down at my feet.

CHEEPER-CHEEPER TAPE, says the Cheeper-Cheeper Tape Bird.

"Your wife work?"

"My girlfriend, yeah." I reach my hands around and massage the back of my neck. The cicadas wind back their clocks in preparation for the afternoon rush.

"Cats run round here," the woman says, pointing at the opening in the fence. "Every which-away. Up trees, under bushes. There a pattern, but you got to see every cat at the same time. But then cats see people seeing cats and that ain't right." She sighed and sat back. "A conundrum. Of course, might could reverse. Cats see people. If cats can see every people at the same time, they see a pattern. We think cats hiding, but cats conferencing about human people. Hotep, you got Pats? Walking the banquette with that bag a bourbon?"

"Pats?" I'm still imagining Free Cookie presenting her findings at a conference of cats. Another PowerPoint. Every cat yawns. "Pats. Middle-aged, balding, usually drunk? Friends with the Strickland Brothers."

"Damn pervert," she says. "Damn pervert."

"I suppose."

The woman begins a series of leg stretches. To accomplish this on the bench, she rests her left leg across my lap. My upbringing didn't really prepare me for older women throwing legs across my lap. Her pink yoga shorts outline her pelvic muscles.

The song descends into a chaotic saxophone solo. The rest of the band tries to play something orderly, but then the trumpet speeds off into a solo if its own.

"Some men ain't perverted, but Pats," she says, "Pats' a damn pervert. Now them hairdressers down the way, they nice. Cats get under they place and have kittens."

"How many do you suppose?"

She stretches her legs widely, then leans over the left leg. She might have been a dancer in her youth. Her muscles flow easily over bone, transforming into whatever shape she needs in the moment.

"Hard to say. Cats ain't last long out here. Coyotes, mange. Round them up. Gotta put the bad ones down, bless their hearts. Cats ain't last long."

"That's awful," I agree.

No cats have shown themselves this whole time. The older woman stops speaking for a moment and concentrates on her stretch. I move my tongue around my mouth. My gums taste salty and dry.

"You sure you won't drink?" she asks. "I got pop."

"No thanks," I tell her.

The older woman fumbles in her shorts and produces a key, which unlocks the red cooler under the bench. It's a small cooler, perhaps large enough for a six-pack and a sandwich, bolted to the bench, and locked. I suppose that makes sense, as much sense as an older woman doing her stretching routine out here. While she's rooting around, I get up and look through the dollhouse library. I expect - I don't know what I expect – but I find Christian easy-reading self-help books, a David Foster Wallace novel, a few tattered classics in paperback, and a lad mag, one of those things that appeals to twenty-something bros who still wear Axe Body Spray. The cover story claims they've discovered the Last Arm Workout You'll Ever Need. I flip through the magazine. The writer's byline says he graduated from the same school I graduated from. I look again, and recognize the writer. Ethiopia Jackson.

I've known Jackson forever. We were the only two black writers in our graduate program. When we all introduced ourselves at the department social, everyone made a performance of being awkward and shy, as if writers can't really be writers unless we're awkward and shy. Ethiopia Jackson has never been awkward or shy. He introduced himself by saying, "Imagine if Indiana Jones was better-looking and taller, with a big black...hat. That's me.," Half the MFA program slept with him by the end of the week. We were roommates. I counted.

I flip to the story and see his photo: Ethiopia Jackson with the biggest shit-eating grin in history, bald now, doing pushups on top of a naked blonde laying on the floor, smiling mischievously, her front side hidden by a white bearskin rug growling mutely at the camera. I put the magazine back in the little dollhouse, then sit down to look at a complete and utter lack of cats.

The older woman finds what she's looking for and re-locks the cooler. She takes off her Lycra shirt and mops sweat from her torso. I guess all sports bras have to fit tightly or they won't work. Did I know older women can look like that? Probably not. Have I ever seen an older woman with her shirt off?

Probably not. Have I seen my girlfriend this undressed, this loose and carefree, in a long time? Probably not.

Sitting there, sandwiched between the sunlight and the river, I've soaked my t-shirt from the shoulders down. She opens her beer with a pop and takes a long swig with her eyes closed and sweat running from her neck to her chest.

"What you teach at your fancy school?" the attractive old woman asks.

"English," I say. "Composition, literature, a few other courses."

"Really?"

"Yeah.,"

"Play ball?"

I sigh. "No, I didn't."

"Look like a ball player."

"Everyone around here is obsessed with football," I say.

"You ain't, Hotep?"

I think about the possibility. "No," I say. "I'm not into football.,"

"English?"

"Yes," I say.

"I hated taking English," she says.

Everyone says that. "Everyone says that," I say.

"Teaching your thing or just your day job?"

I see myself in tiny shorts watching Adrian drive away to work. I change the subject. "How old are you?"

"Ha!" The attractive old woman puts her leg in my lap again, rotates her torso, stretches her arms upwards, and then leans forward, slowly, until her chest and chin touch her leg and her hands rest in my lap. She turns her head to the side.

"Take my hands," she says.

I take her hands.

"Pull," she says.

Her hands draw the heat out of mine, draw heat from my arms and torso. I can't explain the sensation.

She squeezes. She's stronger than I thought.

"Pull."

Right. I pull. Her brown breasts bulge out on the sides of her bra.

"Look here, Hotep."

"Why do you call me Hotep?"

"Cause you Hotep."

"What the hell's a Hotep?" I ask, louder than I intended.

"Don't you know?"

"No, I don't know," I say. My volume control sticks one notch above normal.

"You and me, we got bigger concerns."

"We?"

The attractive old woman sits up. "Ain't you supposed to be looking for your cat instead of staring at my tits?"

I turn my head.

"Go on, stare," she continues. "I won't tell Adrian."

"Oh-kay lady," I say. How does she know Adrian? "I should be going now."

"Knew you clocking. Every woman know you clocking. Ain't like we don't know men be clocking. We feel you looking. Sometimes we say shit, sometimes we don't."

I open my mouth. Suddenly I see slide show images - mothers at the grocery store, colleagues in staff meetings, students at the gym turning, pulling an open shirt closed, turning slightly away right or left. Black, white, Latina, all sorts of women avoiding my look. And I see shimmering women laughing, hanging clothes on a line, chatting with friends, singing in Okahika, the place Randolph calls home.

"Tell a story," she says. The images vanish.

"What?" I say.

"Tell me a story. You teach literature," she says, and I feel pretentious and silly, "so tell me a story." She picks up her beer and takes another long drink.

I nod in a noncommittal sort of way and look, again, at the so-called place where cats hang out. I feel like an idiot. Like an exposed, pervy idiot staring at old lady tits on a bench. Not one cat has crossed my path.

Something in me unwinds. I close my eyes as if I'm falling asleep, with a hat pulled low over my head and an ice-cold beer in the crook of my arm. Sunlight soaks into my skin, warms the sweat pooling in my socks, pushes past my eyelids, and finally rests on my retina, lighting up my optic nerve, and bouncing all the way into my brain, the tiniest of tingling sensations. Delicate insects land on me to catch their breath. In and out. In and out.

The attractive older woman crumples her can. "Tell a story later. Take a nap. I see your cat, I wake you up," she says softly.

My head rolls forward. The world goes silent. The cicadas must be exhausted from running the clock of the world all day, and the Cheeper-Cheeper Tape bird probably ate a big meal before his nap. What if the Cheeper-Cheeper Tape bird ate the cicadas? I hadn't thought of that. That's a lot of cicadas.

Nothing makes a sound, not the attractive older woman next to me, not the wind or the river. Not even a car racing by in the distance.

I think about this attractive older woman. What if I actually do know her? I don't think I do. Know her. I want to open each door of my memory with a woman inside and see if she's there, but I don't think remembering will be that easy. Somebody once said that if dismember means taking the body apart, then remember means putting the body back together.

"Yes," the attractive older woman says. "Put it back together."

She's the haint in my house; she arrived before me. She's the plate that jumps from the counter and shatters on its own.

"You sleep?" the attractive older woman asks so faintly I wonder if I imagined her voice. "You sleep?"

"I'm awake," I reply.

"Put your head in my lap before you fall."

My body tilts over until my head rests on her thighs. Nothing like this has ever happened to me before. I don't know what to think. I wonder what I would say if Adrian found us here like this, and then I decide not to worry. I'll tell her the truth: the attractive older woman's voice sounds different, deeper, slower with my eyes closed, and I'm trying to figure out why. She sounds like someone I know.

"Can I talk?" the attractive older woman asks. "I'll talk quiet. You just listen. Fall asleep if you want."

"Sure," I tell her.

She strokes my forehead gently. The world grows darker and fainter until the only thing that exists is my breathing and her voice and her fingertips.

"Some people see, some don't," she says.

"See what?"

She places three fingers across my lips. "Wrong question, Hotep," she says. "Keep your eyes closed."

I nod. Her fingers smell like cinnamon. She takes her hand from my lips and wraps it around my throat. I swallow involuntarily.

"I'm a leap from the ground and never return," she says. "We want to fly. We see flying, understand it, but we don't believe. Maybe someone pull the magic carpet out and we fall? Ain't so bad."

It's not?

"What if they pull the carpet and we stay up? How we get back down? How we eat up there? Everyone need someplace solid, Hotep. Everyone need to go home."

The woman adjusts her legs under me.

"Too much thinking. A conundrum. Nothing to do, thoughts fly off and don't always come back. The moment,

Hotep, that's what it is. Ain't as scared of flying or falling as that moment when we choose up or down" Right as she says this, the attractive older woman takes her fingers from my throat and opens another beer.

Psst, goes the can.

"It's fine," she says. "I'm watching on Free Cookie. Don't worry. Sleep. My eyes are open. I see your cat, I wake you up. Get some rest. Your cat be here any minute. All the cats hang out here. See what you want, Hotep. See Free Cookie coming closer. She prowling through the grass, she hunting, she deadly, she stalking her victim. She getting closer, closer. See her?"

The sun on my eyelids inverts all my imagined images. I only see Free Cookie as a cat-shaped blur with brightly lit edges, walking through an x-ray world of grassy shapes. When I try to recall our cat, her features separate: a stripe over here, a tail over there. My Free Cookie resembles an exposed negative. The personality remains, but the basics go AWOL.

I can't bother trying to stay awake. I shouldn't fight the inevitable. I should go with the flow. My body feels soft and heavy in the afternoon sun, slumped into the wooden bench. I'm on the hub of the clock of the world. The cicadas keep it moving until the Cheeper-Cheeper Tape bird devours them, and then more cicadas reset the clock, and the Cheeper-Cheeper Tape bird eats them again, and again. While they're gone, everything stops except me. Even the river stops flowing while I grow into a new old shape, my feet lift from the ground, and I burst through the sky, never to return, going, flying past the confines of this planet into the solar system, gawking at the little green aliens who need ships to fly, while the cicadas get back to work for as long as they can, day after day.

The old woman places her fingertip on my lips and traces a pattern I can't make out. Down, across, squiggly marks. Down, across, squiggly marks. A cool quiet liquid darkness leaks from a cracked basin into my mind. The liquid spreads and Free Cookie skips lightly ahead so her paws won't get wet. There you are, I think, there you are. Without a sound, she trots off, looking for higher ground.

Where does she go?

I have no idea.

Maybe you missed the one little thing everyone else figured out, she says.

BEN

Go Home, Ben Hotep. Ben Hotep, Go Home.

As a child, my parents insisted on taking me to church at least once a week, often twice or three times. They both came up out of the deep South in the 60's. They found out, eventually, that God had indeed given them more than they could bear. Dad maybe wanted to become a deacon or a minister, but we never stayed anyplace long enough to accumulate social power. On the other hand, my mother wanted actual power. Holy Power. Sanctified, speaking-in-tongues, snake-charming, you-are-healed-in-the-name-of-Jesus power. Deep down, she resented the socials, the prayer meetings, the choir rehearsals, the plate dinners, and all the subordinate work that women performed while men played and prayed. She wanted to preach and teach others how to behave. Or maybe not. We don't get along, and I can't say I understand my mother very well. I love her, but I don't get her and she doesn't get me.

One Sunday, when I was about 12 or so, we attended some tiny church on the outskirts of Who Knows, USA. We moved around a lot. St. Martin's Missionary Baptist Church of Dayton, or Christ United AME Zion of Tallahassee? St. Someone of Something in Somewhere. The order of events went like this: Sunday School. Church Services. Praise and Worship. Call to Worship. Doxology. Choir (three songs). Pastoral Prayer. Choral Response (one song). Recognition of Visitors. Announcements. Tithes and Offerings. Prayer by Pastor. Choir (one song). Deacon's Prayer. Choir (one song). Scripture Reading. Sermon. Invitation. Altar Call (with music). Benediction. Postlude.

If we arrived after 8am, we were late. If we left before 1pm, my parents complained that the church wasn't right with God. If the sermon lasted less than 45 minutes, my parents made excuses for the preacher: his kid went to jail again, or his wife left him, or his Cadillac had a flat. Once, Dad hustled us out mid-service because a woman played a tambourine. Any instruments besides piano and organ disrespected the house of God, in his opinion. On this Sunday, the pastor – another name I can't remember – shouted and chanted, danced, sweat, exhorted us all to devote our lives to Jesus and something in me changed. I felt pulled, drawn up, as if an invisible hand gripped me from inside. The room filled with light, illuminating goodness, kindness, charity, worn across human bodies like clothing. When the Pastor invited us to stand, step forward, and get transformed into something new, I rose, ready to feel the Holy Water strip away my sins – until my mother shot her arm across my chest and shoved me roughly back into the pew. The light faded and everything vanished.

I thought God would punish her, or punish me. She subverted God's will in His house and I had been too weak to stand. But nothing happened. I was too old to cry. We just went on. The preacher never noticed that one of his flock didn't come. The choir kept singing. Dad kept praying and nodding, praying and nodding. Old ladies fanned themselves. Babies cried and kids ran around. Ushers took money in brass plates lined with red felt. The sun shone and the world revolved as it had before. Nothing happened; nothing had happened. We pretended nothing had happened. My mother never explained why she did what she did. She never apologized. Part of my brain said, aha, if God doesn't punish me, then God can't exist. That makes sense. Everything has to make sense.

I did get baptized about three years later at a better (more affluent, more suburban, more politically powerful) church. A proper black church with the right connections, where kids received Ivy League scholarships and local politicians posed for photos. The church elders took me – I was 14 by that time – plus a few other teenagers and a woman in her late 40's, to the banks of the Hudson on a bleak March morning. We were all freezing. One by one, they took us into the shallows, prayed, then dipped us, arms crossed, in and out of the river. Everyone else came out wet and gasping, yet aglow, grinning, joyous. Families celebrated. I entered the water dry and cold. I exited wet and cold.

Maybe that's where my life went wrong. Maybe some things can only happen once. You take them or they're gone. Maybe that's the one little thing. Or maybe not. You're looking for a cat one day but you find a half-dressed old woman, some rope, and a bench in what used to be a place.

The rope. That was my dream. Gym class, fourth grade, 1978 or so. Looking up at the ceiling, where the gym teacher attaches a thick rope to the rafters. Anyone who makes it to the top gets to ring a bell. We live in some town in far upstate New York, way out in the sticks. Most of my teachers have never met a black person before. Some have never *seen* a black person before, except on TV.

"Hughes!" the coach yells. "Get on up there." Kids make monkey sounds. I can't climb the rope. I can't complain to my parents about how the kids treat me at school, unless I want to hear another lecture on MLK or about how the white man needed to learn tolerance. I can't teach anyone tolerance in powder blue gym shorts with yellow stripes around the edges. "Just learn to ignore them," my parents say. I never learn to ignore them. I only learn to stop complaining about them.

"Hughes," the coach yells. "Get up that rope." If I climb, the monkey sounds will never stop. If I don't climb, the coach will put me in the sissy line with the other boys who don't reach the top. I decide to climb half way. The rope feels thick and prickly against my body, arms and legs and feet inchworming upwards. I reach the halfway mark and I feel that inner grip again, some irresistible urge to keep climbing. I reach hand over hand, up, up, up. I reach the top but the bell is missing. I can't find it. I feel rough, wet wood. Water drips down my shirt. A splinter pierces my hand. Blood turns the rope slippery, I grip harder but I'm slipping. The sky stretches to the horizon. I hear gulls and sailcloth flapping in the wind. I look around and see a long, wooden keel partially blocking the sun, dripping with stale water. I can just make out a figure – a woman, a tall, curvy woman – standing near me. She turns to look at me and I see her feet in midair, supported by nothing. Just then, Free Cookie runs up the bloody rope. Her claws sink into my bare legs. I lose my grip and fall.

I wake on the hard ground. After a few seconds, I realize I never transitioned from sleeping to waking. I didn't get the nice, slow, drowsy time when I'm awake with eyes closed, when I perceive the world one sense at a time: the Cheeper-Cheeper Tape bird, the last cicada singing quietly, sunlight through the side windows, the warmth of Adrian's breath curling around my neck, her air filling my lungs and going out and coming back in. This was nothing like that. This was more like some cosmic entity had been chatting with a friend and said:

'Hey, you know that guy Ben? Did you turn him on?'

'Ben Hughes?' the other entity says. 'I thought today was your day.'

So the first entity says, 'You're right. My bad.'

Then it flips my switch.

The attractive old woman is gone. She must have locked the cooler under the park bench and closed the little dollhouse library doors. What a crazy day. What an insane day. The jogger - the attractive old woman – I never asked her name – The Through. What did Randolph call it? Hotep. No, I'm Hotep. I'm not Hotep. I've never had a day like this in my life. In-sane. None of today makes sense. I'm a logical person. I like things to make sense. The sun hangs low in the trees and shade covers me up to the waist. My watch says it's 4:32. I massage my jaw for a few seconds, stand, and take a look around. Everything looks the same as it did when I arrived. Hole in the fence, bench, pile of tires, rope, an old car, trees, shrubs, cicadas, weeds, birds, bats. No cats, no woman, no cats.

I lope about aimlessly, letting my legs and feet wake up again while I search for some sign of a cat nearby. Ten minutes later, there's nothing. No cats, no woman, no cats. Nothing moves but me. My leg hums as if I'm getting a phone call, but I'm not. I heard a podcast about the syndrome. Ringxiety. We're anxious about getting so many calls that we invent more, or we're anxious about not getting calls, so we invent more. Another thing I'll add to the list for today. I look down the riverbanks as far as I can see, and under the trestle, all across The Through. There's no sign of anyone around, only the sun slowly sinking beneath the pine trees. There's nothing to do but cross back over and go home.

I don't know what to do now. I had a weird day and one of those falling dreams. I woke when I hit the ground. That all makes sense. Sure. But the feeling that I've missed something comes back stronger than ever. The cicadas are silent. Everything is silent. I hear nothing, no birds, no wind. Perhaps the world forgot it exists. I should go home and write something about the jogger and the woman and the cat and the cicadas and the Cheeper-Cheeper Tape bird. Nothing comes to mind right away. Besides, no one wants to read stories from a failed adjunct professor. Most people have never even seen a cicada anyway. One of my professors in grad school told me it's hard to write about a train wreck while the train is still wrecking. But writing today feels like a big commitment. Once a story starts, I have to finish it to the end. The only way to avoid getting sucked in is to never start at all. But I'm on that train already and the conductor just punched my ticket. No refunds.

Now the world wakes up, just a little. I hear a rhythmic creaking in the trees, like someone tied a gigantic red kite onto the tree with a thick piece of rope, which sways as the kite moves above the clouds. One of those old-fashioned, diamond-shaped kites, red, with yellow bows in the tail. Or maybe I just have rope on the brain. Probably a branch rubbing against another branch. I should move just in case it falls.

My throat tingles where the attractive old woman touched me. I feel her fingers cross my throat, down, across, squiggly marks. Maybe my throat has Ringxiety too. I grab my phone and unwind the earphones. Maybe I should block bizarre events for the rest of the day. I stretch and get an image of myself running around Northport with a Do Not Disturb hotel sign hung around my neck. In this town, everyone would come up and say, 'Hey Ben, where you get that Do Not Disturb sign? Motel 6? You been to Motel 6? They got good breakfast.' And then just keep talking while I wonder if they really don't understand what Do Not Disturb means or if they're just screwing with me.

I pull my phone out. A message tells me I've downloaded the podcast Adrian wanted, the one about cicadas. I don't remember doing that, but here it is. I decide to listen on the way home. I might as well learn something today. I'm unusually stiff. My quads and calves feel sore, and my hips feel like I've been clenching a ball between my legs all afternoon. I'll take a slow run, then go home and make dinner.

Magnolia flowers scent the air. We have other flowers – red azalea petals, white hydrangea, and little pink flowers that come up in our lawn and everywhere else. I might smell any one of those, but I assume I'm smelling magnolia since those flowers are bigger. Isn't that strange? Shouldn't make a difference. I walk around the bench a few times, looking for whatever's making that noise. I can't see anything, so I walk to the fence. The city should mow out here. I don't see anything here either, nothing rubbing the fence or a tree, nothing moving at all. Weird. Maybe I imagined the sound, or maybe I heard the sound when I dreamt about the rope and the memory persisted. Insisted.

Anyway.

I walk towards the hole in the fence and trip over a thick hemp rope at my feet, trailing across the bench and the little library, leading up into an old silk cotton tree. An urge to climb seizes me. When was the last time I climbed a tree? Never? I could say that I want to untie the rope and throw it away, or think Free Cookie could be hiding up there, but the truth is I don't know why I want to climb this tree. I look up the trunk and see thick, leafy branches spaced fairly evenly. The trunk is smooth and warm to the touch but massive, reassuring in a way. This is not some junky tree that will collapse under my weight. No warranty needed. I jump to the lowest branch and pull myself up. I'm out of shape. My arms strain and pull, but I can't get my legs up to the branch. I'm a pool of sweat now or maybe it's started to rain. Drops tap my forehead. This is ridiculous. I don't know what I was thinking. I jump down. I pull on the rope a few times but it's stuck. Whoever tied it will just have to come get it back.

The wind picks up and the light dims. I don't remember hearing about a storm today, but the weather changes quickly around here. The cicadas and the Cheeper-Cheeper Tape Bird have fallen silent again, which they always do before a big storm. I look around one more time - if Cookie gets hurt by a falling branch - I don't want to think about it. Cookie's not here. That rope noise starts again, then again. Louder. Again. The wind rattles every leaf like a woman shaking a tambourine. I hear wood crack and splinter, and scramble to the fence just before a massive silk cotton tree branch falls and crushes the park bench.

Something juts from the treetops. A long straight branch, ash black against the deep sky. That can't be a branch, it's too straight. A pole of some sort, not straight up but leaning forward and—moving. Or the tree is moving. The massive tree seems to recede back and leave this thing behind, this ashen pole leaning forwards. The pole attaches to more wood, all that same black-ash color. It's hard to make out details. More poles appear, sticking straight up now, with crossbeams hanging off them like the masts of an old sailing ship. Exactly like the masts of an old sailing ship. The pole moves forward, attached to a long black hull, trailing the think rope I saw before. The hull pushes through the top branches of the tree. More crash down. I can't move, can't think, can't even breathe. The ship descends. Now I can see most of it: hull, masts, wheel, rudder, rope. It's close, maybe 40 feet away. A fierce wind pitches down and it flies right at me. It's going to crush me, I think. It's going to crush me and there's nothing I can do. 30 feet. Everything stops but the wind and the ship. It's so close I can smell sweat and blood and pus and shit soaked into the floorboards, sharp, acrid gunpowder, melted metal. The ship rattles. 20 feet. I hear chains. They sound like a bad high school production of A Christmas Carol. Marley, is that you? I giggle and I can't stop. This is how I die, I think. Giggling at the flying ship about to crush me. 10 feet. The ship flies right at me and levels off at the last moment. Instead of flying into me, it flies over me, creaks, groans, and stops. Saltwater drips from the ship onto my head and trickles down into my shoes.

I want to breathe, but the stench makes my eyes water. I don't know what's happening to me. I must be hallucinating. I'm going crazy. Or that attractive old woman roofied me, she—

Ben.

—Slipped something in my drink, but I never had a drink, so she—

"Ben."

—Must have injected me or—

"Ben. Ben, baby, come back."

My heart thumps hard inside my chest and everything that stopped comes back. The cicadas chirp, the birds sings, the sun peeks around the corners of the ship. But it's still there. I whirl around and see the old woman standing next to the fence. She waves at me. "Ben," she says, "Ben, come on honey. Take a step towards me."

I don't move.

"Ben," she says, "take a step."

My entire body feels foreign, like a marionette under someone else's control. I lift one awkward leg and set it down. I lift the other.

"That's it Ben. Come on."

I place my leg down and forward. My weight shifts forward. I move. The ship creaks. I lift my other leg and place it down and forward. My weight shifts forward. I move. The ship groans. I lift my legs again and faster, moving towards the old woman and the fence. The ship moves with me. Terrified, I look back and stumble to the left. The ship moves to the left. Now I run. My body has forgotten how to run. I cannot run. I am a jumble of moving parts lurching towards the fence. I point at her. "You," I say, "you—"

"Althea," the attractive old woman says.

"What?"

"Say my name," she says. "Althea."

"You did—Althea—what did you—"

"Ben, come on! Keep running."

I fall again and the ship dips so low I can't stand without hitting my head. I scramble on my hands and knees in the dirt, crying, panting like a dog, heart thumping, yammering senseless sounds.

"Come on Ben, come on," Althea yells. She waves at me like I need to hurry and I think there's a damn ship floating above my head, of course I need to hurry. I crab-crawl to the fence. The ship hovers above. Then, with all the deliberate carefulness of a mother with her newborn baby, *Yemaya* tilts, points her prow downwards, and spears me through the heart.

Her prow pins me to the ground like an insect on display. I cannot speak, cannot breathe. My arms and legs flail like a beetle on its back. I am an insect. I am an object of curiosity to the universe. My life is a teachable moment, nothing more, a brief example for study.

Was. My life was.

I'm going to die correcting verb tenses.

Althea squats over me. She grabs the prow with both hands and pushes. Nothing happens. Althea breathes quickly and pushes with her legs and feet, her arms and her back, her stomach, her cervix, her neck. *Yemaya* moves back and up, easing the pressure in my chest. Althea pushes and pushes. The prow pulls back and releases me. "Go, Ben!"

Go.

"Go home, Ben Hotep." Althea pushes against the ship until it levels in the air. "She ain't follow past the fence."

I can't, I can't, I can't.

"Ben Hotep, go home." Althea picks up the thick rope I'd pulled before. "Ain't she your cat?" she says.

Free Cookie trots across my legs and on through the hole in the fence, tail up and twitching. She's heading home. I crawl after her. A weight leaves my chest as soon as I pass the fence. I stand up and feel my chest. Everything is where it should be. My heart beats and I take a few deep breaths, relishing the sound of air in my lungs.

Free Cookie walks ahead. I know I should follow her, but I have to look back before I go. Past the fence, Althea tows *Yemaya* back to the cotton tree, an ash black silhouette in the red sun.

Cicadas, The Clock of the World

ANNOUNCER: If you haven't seen them, you've heard their unmistakable sound. Cicadas. Often mistaken for locusts, these insects emerge once every 13 or 17 years to eat, mate, and die. And sing, using tiny organs called tymbals. It's the sound of summer in Alabama.

According to author and etymologist Jean Fontana, cicadas run the world. More specifically, genetically distinct populations or "broods" as they're called—23 in North America alone—regulate the timing of plant, bird, and animal growth. Cicada larvae prune trees and bushes when they emerge, but rarely cause any significant damage. More importantly, cicadas are an important food source for Alabama wildlife, including fish, raccoons and other rodents, frogs, reptiles of all kinds, spiders, and even other insects. Without cicadas eating and getting eaten, Fontana says, Alabama wouldn't be able to sustain biodiversity.

Here in Alabama, Brood XIX (19) will emerge this year, then go to sleep. Brood 19 is composed of four distinct genetic varieties and covers everything from East Texas to the Carolinas, including Alabama. They hatch on a 13-year cycle. The next emergence in this area will be in 2024, but local varieties hatch every year. Dr. Fontana, can you help us make some sense of this? How do we have cicadas every year if they only emerge once every 13 years?

FONTAINE: It's Fontaine. Well, two reasons. The first is a couple of cicada species are annuals.

ANNOUNCER: Annuals in the plant sense?

FONTAINE: I suppose you could say that. Their active life cycle lasts about a month, but they rarely live more than 2 weeks after mating. In fact, the Diceroprocta viridifascia or salt marsh cicada—

ANNOUNCER: Now you said there's another reason?

FONTAINE: Um, yes. Species from other parts of the country can wind up here on trucks and cars. And a small percentage of 13-year brood cicadas don't go into hibernation on time. We're still figuring that out.

ANNOUNCER: Maybe you should give them a glass of warm milk. [Laughs] Is there any way for farmers and gardeners to keep cicadas from eating their plants?

FONTAINE: That's a common misunderstanding. Locusts will destroy gardens and crops, but cicadas and locusts aren't the same species, not even close.

ANNOUNCER: Look at the time! Let's take a break for station identification.

[Pre-recorded message plays.]

ANNOUNCER: Thanks for listening. We're talking to Dr. Jean Fontana, author of *Cicadas: The Clock of the World*. Dr. Fontana—

FONTAINE: Call me Jean.

ANNOUNCER: ...Dr. Fontana, you said that cicadas run the world. What did you mean by that?

FONTAINE: Cicadas are nature's timekeepers. Their emergence enables many other species to eat and reproduce. If a species has lost its food supply due to environmental factors, the cicada can provide critical nutrition. But more importantly, cicadas maintain a clock of sorts, a natural clock. Think of it like seasons. We have summer, winter, spring, and cicadas. Cicada clocks are more complex than watches, and so we didn't understand them for a long time. We've still got the local varieties. Think of it this way: the local cicadas - annuals, to use your metaphor - keep the clock running so to speak, through regular maintenance: eating small plants and getting eaten in turn. Brood 19 emerges to reset the whole clock.

ANNOUNCER: Fascinating. So why do cicadas make that sound? Is it a mating call?

FONTAINE: Yes. The males sing to attract females, and the females respond.

ANNOUNCER: How does that work? Do the females go to whoever's the loudest, or is there some other criteria involved?

FONTAINE: It's something of a duet. But once mating starts, it lasts 4-5 days.

ANNOUNCER: Days! Mad respect. Now I also understand that you're something of a cicada trivia aficionado.

FONTAINE: Well, I wrote a book—

ANNOUNCER: I remember you mentioned something about cicada poetry?

FONTAINE: Yes, several poets have dedicated poems to cicadas, usually talking about the immense silence when they go back into hibernation. My favorite is a Chinese poem from 1056.

ANNOUNCER: Can you read it for us?

FONTAINE: Sure.

Here was a thing that cried upon a treetop
sucking the shrill wind
To wail it back in a long whistling note ...
    And who seemed to miss them
when they vanished ...
Again your voice, cicada ...
       ... as suddenly as it began
suddenly ceases.

ANNOUNCER: Thank you. Jean Fontana's new book, *Cicadas: The Clock of the World*, will be on sale tonight at his lecture in Smith Hall on the University campus. 7 pm and open to the public.

[Note: This broadcast was edited for length and to correct Jean Fontaine's profession. Dr. Fontaine is a professor of entymology, not etymology as previously stated.]

ADRIAN

The Mother
and the Baby
Tied to
Her Back

I tapped the End Call button three times. The phone froze and left Ben's face half-faded on my screen. He looks like Ashy Larry. I smiled thinking about Ben running around in his underwear playing dice. He would never do that, but he should. Monday, Wednesday, and Friday, he gets up in the morning, shaves, dresses like a grown man, picks up his briefcase and drives to class. When he writes, he just sits around on the couch. Half the time he's watching TV or taking a walk. I've tried talking to him, but he says I'm not a writer and I don't understand the process.

Writers write, Ben. I understand the process.

"Another fight?" Gloria asked. One of my partners stood in the doorway of my office, framed in an oval of late summer sunlight beaming through the windows. Gloria is older than the rest of us, short, with a solid build and salt-of-the-earth face that makes clients feel their money is safe. We met on the first day of Statistics for Business. She walked up to me and said, "Bet you never met a 45 year old great-grandma before," then explained that she'd had a daughter at 15, who had a daughter at 14, who had a daughter at 16. They still lived together in the trailer park, one generation after another. I liked her instantly.

"I tried to get Ben interested in a job," I said.

"Let me guess, he didn't go for it."

"I don't know what's happened to him," I said. "When I first moved here, I don't know, he seemed like he had it together. He had so many plans I couldn't keep up."

"Did he ever pull them off?" Gloria asked.

"Not really. He applied for jobs, started a book, wrote for some website. But then things tapered off, and he stopped writing. Unless he's grading, he just sits around. He won't even get a haircut now."

"What was the job?"

"What job?" I asked.

"Hey, Miss Gloria." Edward stuck his head into my office. About a week into our partnership, we realized that Ed had joined up because of his crush on Gloria. He's slightly older than her but never married, a trustee at his church. He dresses well, but there's always something not quite right: his tie doesn't match, or he's put on one brown sock and one blue sock. Definitely in need of a woman's touch. Ed asked Gloria to marry him at least once a day, and she always found a way to say no. Maybe one day she'll say yes.

"Hey Edward," Gloria said.

"When you gonna marry me Miss Gloria?" Ed asked.

Gloria sipped a latte that she got from the coffee and juice bar on the next block. She looked him up and down. "The day you show me a paper from the doctor that says you got 24 hours to live."

Edward's face sagged. He clutched his chest and staggered around like Fred G. Sanford. "It's the big one! It's the big one! I'm coming, Elizabeth!"

Gloria and I laughed. "Out!" I said, "out of my office."

"But I— "

"Out." Edward mock-pouted and left. Gloria watched him go back to his office, still smiling.

"You are glowing," I said.

"Quiet. This ain't about me. We're talking about you. Now what about this job, the job you tried to get Ben into?"

"The job, right. I made it up."

"What?"

"He looked so pathetic. I thought hearing about a job would cheer him up. I just wanted him to do something besides sitting and sulk. It shouldn't bother me, but seeing him on the couch pisses me off."

"What were you gonna do if he got interested?"

"One of our clients must have something."

"Adrian!"

"I know, I know. It never would have worked."

"No, Adrian, your hand," Gloria said. "You're bleeding."

I looked at my left hand. A long slash ran diagonally across my palm. Blood dripped onto the desk.

"I must have cut myself," I said.

Gloria hurried out of the office. "Ed!" Gloria yelled. "Edward! Do we have a First Aid kit?"

A cicada burst out of my hand, crawled up my arm and onto my back, latched onto the space between my skull and neck, squirmed, pushed, dug, until it created a cocoon between my bones. The cicada hummed in contentment.

I brushed the back of my head. Stop! Stop!

Startled, Edward said to Gloria, "First Aid? Yes? No?"

"Which is it Ed?"

"I don't know where it is," Ed said.

The humming and buzzing grew louder. Soon, I couldn't hear anything else, not Gloria and Ed, not the phones or the cars outside. I opened my mouth to shout and the cicada sang instead, sang sweetness, sang sweetness, vibrating my entire body: bones, blood, cells, molecules, atoms, the space between atoms. My heart beat a rhythm against my breasts. My chin and knees, my ass and calves played an off-beat syncopated pattern. My neck, arms, and thighs sang in harmony. I was the symphony and the conductor. I was the mother and the baby tied to her back, one body split into two. The windows and floors took our song. The building and ground played rhythmic beats while the passing river and clouds sang, shaking the world.

My legs were covered in mud. Everything smelled like soot. I stood in a long line in the wreck of what used to be a hospital maternity ward, all the babies long gone. A poster showed a plump baby nursing and said, "Breast is Best. Breastfeed your baby." My mother must have fed me that way. She must have. We didn't have money for formula. But I can't imagine her opening her shirt and putting my mouth to her nipple, even if I was hungry and she had the only food I could eat. I never cut myself. All the children left. New Orleans played in fast-motion, emptying herself. Children left their playgrounds, friends stopped laughing, birds stopped flying. One solitary bird sat on a ledge. It looked like a pigeon, but it said CHEEPER-CHEEPER. TAPE! CHEEPER-CHEEPER TAPE!

The Cheeper-Cheeper Tape flew into my hair and pecked at the back of my neck. The cicada panicked and tried to burrow through my skull, but the bird plunged its sharp beak inside me and wrestled the cicada out. The buzzing stopped, but too late, too late. Something broke. The Cheeper-Cheeper Tape bird flew to the window and ate the cicada, still alive, soaked in blood.

"Adrian? Oh my God," Gloria said. "Adrian, you fainted."

The dull and hazy edges of the world returned. A low throb replaced the buzzing. Blood soaked my hand. I cut myself. I never cut myself. I'm not that kind of person. I'm stronger than that,. I'm stronger than that, so it never happened. But the song was gone.

"I'm fine," I said. "I'm fine." I opened my eyes and saw a brown, flat surface with parallel lines running across it. Feet ran towards me.

"You're not fine," Gloria said, bending down. "You're on the floor. Did you hit your head?"

Where is the song?

"I'm—ow!" I pushed myself up, and the slash on my hand pushed back. It hurt like hell. How had I done that? Gloria helped me to my chair. Drops of blood covered the desk and the back of my head felt wet.

"I'm gonna call an ambulance," Gloria said.

"No, no," I said. "I'll be fine. I just fainted. I, I must have cut myself while I was talking to Ben. On the folder. And then I tripped."

"That's one hell of a paper cut," Gloria said.

"I'll be fine. I just need a bandage or something."

"Here," Edward said. He brought in our first-aid kit, still wrapped in plastic. "Do you have any scissors?"

"Yes," I said. I meant no. Shit. Scissors. I must have cut myself with the scissors while I was talking to Ben. I don't cut myself. I'm such an idiot. Now they'll know and they'll want to reach out. It's none of their fucking business. I don't care what they say. I don't care if they think their sister, their daughter, granddaughter, ex-girlfriend is like me. I don't give a fuck. I'm not some weak suburban teenager. No one's like me, no one understands, so just leave me the hell alone.

"Found them," Edward said. He took a pair of scissors from the cup on my desk and cut the packaging off. While Edward and Gloria unpacked the supplies, I stole a look at the scissors. Clean. Not a drop of blood on them. If I hadn't cut myself with scissors, what did I use? I didn't even remember doing it. I remembered my skin peeling back, like my hand cut itself without me.

My partners found the alcohol wipes and a roll of gauze.

"Let's get this wrapped up," said Gloria. "Then you're going home for the day."

"Or for a drink," Edward said.

"A drink sounds real good," I said. "Like for real, for real."

"Looks dirty," Gloria said.

"Yeah," Edward agreed. "You should wash up. Want me to get you some water?"

"Edward," I said. "I can wash my own hands. Give me the gauze. I'll wrap it up in the bathroom." I stood up, a little shaky, and then walked to the bathroom. I turned on the water and let it run. I couldn't decide what was worse, wrapping my hand as-is, then having the 'talk' with Ben at home. Ben saying 'why didn't you tell me' like I owed him. Or put my hand in the water and take my chances.

I looked at my hand, and saw a pattern. A long, bloody X crisscrossed my left palm. Painful welts rose in each quadrant. I felt like I could read them. Maybe they wouldn't make sense to anyone else, but they made sense to me. The top one read 8-29. The bottom one said 1-2. The left said AD, and the right had an O. I didn't know what it meant, but I knew what it was. A Katrina Cross. The mark rescuers put on houses after the flood.

I pressed my hand to my heart.

The back of my head still felt wet. I turned the back of my head towards the mirror and tried to look, but I couldn't see anything. The water ran. I looked at myself in the mirror. My face, my eyes, all looked back. I'd almost been expecting someone else. I would have welcomed someone else who could take this body and leave. I didn't want it anymore. I used my good hand to wipe my face. I decided to put my bad hand in the water. Ok. Go. Go. On the count of three. One, two, three. Ok, countdown. Ten. Nine. Eight. Seven. Six. Five. Four. Three. Two. One.

One.

Go.

One.

Like diving off the high board.

One.

You mine little mama.

A thick finger jammed up my anus.

Fast bitch.

Marcel I'm bloody and I'm counting down to oneoneoneoneoneoneoneoneoneoneone water overflowed the sink and drenched me head to toe. I looked at my hand. The bloody mark had left and, like the cat, might never be seen again. My skin looked exactly like it normally did. I couldn't feel a scar or any lingering pain. Not on my hand. I still felt Marcel's finger inside me, but that was not new. I felt him every day. There was nothing I could do except turn off the water.

I wrapped my hand in the bandage anyway. We had a mop in the bathroom closet. I found it, but by then all the water had drained away and my clothes were dry again. We cleaned the blood off my desk and we had to reprint a few reports but everything was fine, fine, okay, just fine.

Like the Wanderer, the Sun Gone Down

I've been crossed, as the old people liked to call it. Marked in blood that washes away like it was never there. I don't even know what that means.

I left the office just after five, promising to take care of myself and call if I needed anything. I didn't know what I needed. Everything. Nothing. I felt hungry, but I'd eaten from every restaurant near our office too many times. I wanted a drink, but my usual bar might have friends or clients hanging out after work and I didn't want to chat.

I decided to drink at home. Ben was (supposed to be) out looking for Cookie, so he wouldn't have dinner ready. I didn't like his cooking anyway, though I never told him. He tried, but I got too much of home in me to enjoy kale and quinoa salad. I wanted real food, down-home food, normal food, New Orleans food, but New Orleans got washed away. New Orleans was never there. We lived a fiction where visiting women exposed their breasts for Made in China plastic, where tourists came hoping someone had died so they could gawk at the funeral. But when we actually died, when the whole damn city died, they left us to rot unmourned, unsung, unloved, uncared. No one came to our funeral. We were the place everyone wanted to go. Until we weren't. We took to shouting. At first just at night, but then daylight shouting. No one was angry, we just started shouting. Where's the hammer, you hungry yet, that sort of thing. Our city lay silent and dead on her back. Shouting took the edge off, made home seem a little less like a graveyard. We had to make the silence back off.

New Orleans was never meant for silence. My whole life and I never heard New Orleans silent. Slow and mournful, happy and quick, sure. Quiet, so quiet I could hear leaves fall. But never silent. New Orleans always had too much to say. But that was then. People have moved back to the neighborhoods, but I haven't spoken to anyone from home since I left. They probably think I'm dead. I'm not. I'm in the here and now, stuck in traffic on the bridge between Tuscaloosa and Northport. I'm hungry and I want a drink. I never understood why a town this small had such bad traffic. Every morning and afternoon, traffic crossing the bridge over the Black Warrior

River comes to a standstill. It's not like people have tons of accidents here. Maybe they're just slow.

Tuscaloosa had this little quirk—at certain times, all the lights went out. Some problem with the power grid, Ben mansplained, but he invents explanations. Can't handle uncertainty. This was one of those days. All the streetlights went dark at once. They shouldn't have made much of a difference during rush hour, but suddenly everything went dark. The sky, the river, the trees all went dark. The sun set but the moon did not rise. I should have turned my lights on, but I didn't. No one else did either. A woman ran past my car, holding out her phone. Then a man did the same thing. Another man wove his motorcycle through the stalled traffic, stopped, and began taking pictures with a real camera. Cicadas started to sing so loud that I felt their vibrations through my feet. I got out, ran to the railing, and looked at the river.

At first, I only saw a dark blot under the water. I stepped closer to the railing. The blot billowed and changed shape, like clouds before a bad storm. Beneath the water, the blot struggled into wakefulness. It moved. It yawed left and right. It pitched its nose upward and slid across the river bottom, heading directly towards me. Schools of tiny silvery fish scattered before a sharp soot cloud moving under the water. A suggestion of sharpness. No eddy or ripple marked its passage, and the strong currents did not push the small cloud downstream. But not so small. As large as a shark. Sharks can't swim in rivers. Can they? Fish darted away from the cloud. Fish too old or slow to flee drifted through the mass and floated belly-up to the surface. A woman screamed. A spar broke the water and stretched into a mast.

"*Yemaya*," someone said, voice trembling. I turned around and saw the older woman from before, the woman who looked like Mama, still dressed in her pink jogging clothes. Even with her back turned, I knew it was her. I'd know her anywhere. Some people stay in your life forever, and some wander in and out, but when they come back, conversations pick up right where they left off. That's how I felt about this woman. I knew we had something to say to each other. Her eyes stared at the growing thing in the water. I wanted to hold her.

"Oh, child," she said. A long, ancient ship emerged from the river. Spar, mast, bow, rail, deck, wheel, rudder, without sails or sailors. Chains rattled. She moved quickly up and out of the water, sailed directly over our heads, then disappeared in low clouds.

"Child, you have to run," she said without moving.

I didn't move. I was too scared to move.

"Adrian, run."

"What was that?"

"*Yemaya*." The old woman takes a long, sobbing breath. "*Yemaya*. Do you remember, when you were a girl, you heard the story about the Flying Africans?"

"Yes, but—" How would she know about granmé and her stories on the porch, out on their farm in the country? "Who are you?" I asked.

She turned to me and I wailed loud and long like a dog kicked in the gut. Mama.

"Mama, you're alive."

"You destroyed our family."

"Mama, I can't."

"You drove Marcel to drink with your lies," she said.

"I never lied!" I said. "You never believed me."

"Always something wrong with you. Knew it from day you born."

"Fuck you!"

"Let me float away in that filthy water. Your own mama! Put a roof over your head and you left!"

"Leave me alone!" I cried. "Just leave."

"You watched Marcel die while I drowned in my own fucking house!"

"Leave me alone!"

"I ain't visiting noways," Mama said, and vanished. I looked around as if she could have hidden somewhere on the bridge, but she left as quickly as she came. Everyone stared at the spot where *Yemaya* vanished into the clouds, but I felt exposed anyway. Cicadas sang again, louder than I ever imagined, loud enough that the bridge vibrated under my feet. The streetlights flickered on. Everyone restarted their cars. Clouds over the river parted and revealed a red sunset.

The photographer on the motorcycle walked over to me. He still had his helmet on. He waved at me and took it off. We'd met before. He was Ben's friend from school, Jackson.

"Hey, it's Adrian!"

"Yeah. Yeah." I remembered his face, his voice, his looks, his arms. A handsome man who'd started to go soft in middle age, but still dressed and acted like he was 25. His shiny red motorcycle screamed midlife crisis. "You're one of Ben's friends."

"Ethiopia Jackson," he said, looking a little disappointed. I remembered him just fine, but I wouldn't let him think so. Jackson (Ethiopia will never cross my lips), believed every woman must love him. He and Ben went way back, but I'd always excused myself when they started talking about the old days.

"Sorry, baby," I said. I showed him my bandaged hand. "I've had a crazy day."

"No doubt, no doubt," he said. "We got ships flying around here."

"Wait, what?" I asked. "You saw it?"

"I took pictures," he said. "I tried, I don't know if they came out. I'm here covering a story." A car honked at us. "But we should get off this bridge. Lemme follow to y'alls place and I'll see if any photos came out."

On the one hand, I didn't want Jackson coming over. I can handle his type on most days but right then, I just wanted to go home and cuddle with Ben on the couch. I'd even eat his crazy food. No talking, no TV, just the two of us, together, comforting each other, and maybe some music. On the other hand, I wanted to see those pictures. And it's rude to turn someone away. And if I looked in the dictionary under "eye candy" I'd find an old picture of Jackson. Not that old.

I restarted my car and took the exit ramp. Jackson followed me down and through our little neighborhood. I scanned the sky, saw nothing but blue. I'd look later where I'd seen the ship before, down by the trestle. The trestle! Shit. I sent Ben down there to look for Free Cookie. I didn't want him running into Mama, whatever she was, until I'd had a chance to explain. What would I say? What could I possibly say that would explain anything that happened today?

I pulled into the driveway and Jackson parked on the street. He left his helmet dangling from a side view mirror. Then he took his camera out of his bag. I started to say no, but he took a picture of me anyway.

"Jackson!"

"Sorry, sorry. I wanted to ask but the light was too perfect," he said. "Here, let me pull up the pic." We stood together as he scrolled through his photos: the football team practicing, the football team working out, blonde sorority girls posing, some generic photos of Tuscaloosa, and the bridge. A black sailing ship floating in mid-air, above the bridge, sailing off into the trees around the bend of the Black Warrior River.

"Damn," he said. "People are gonna think I photoshopped these. And look," he said, "You can see all the lights are off. No sunlight, no moonlight. I shouldn't have captured any image at all. I can't explain that either." I couldn't disagree.

Jackson scrolled to his last photo, the one of me. A halo of red light framed my head and turned my dress almost transparent. My hair looked as if I'd dipped the edges in blood. I looked straight at the camera, and a slight smile started on the sides of my mouth. Frozen in time, my bandaged hand didn't say, 'no' as much as, 'blessings upon you'.

"Whoa," Jackson said. "I should get down and pray."

"Shut up." But my picture asked me to pray too. For a moment, I knew anything I wanted would happen. If I told Jackson to fuck me until I forgot my hand and the water and a flying slave ship, he would. If I told Free Cookie to come home right that moment, she would. If I told Ben to pack our shit and move us to New Orleans, he would. But in that moment, I only wanted my sister, whoever she was, whatever she was, dead or alive, real or imagined, flesh or water, wherever she existed, to come and protect me from Mama and the cicadas and flying ships and the Cheeper-Cheeper Tape Bird.

A black woman jogged down the street and turned towards us. Not Mama again, I thought, not this again. But she didn't look quite like Mama. Younger and taller, but those same hips, that same smile. She waved at us and kept running.

"Damn," Jackson said. "She could be your twin."

"I- I-" I stammered. "I had a sister before, but she—the same day as Mama—" I burst into tears.

"Oh no," Jackson said, "Katrina. I didn't know." He wrapped me in his arms. I let him hold me.

We must have looked like lovers.

After a time, I pulled away from him and wiped my face. "So," I said, "what brings you to town?"

"I'm on assignment for my magazine," Jackson said. "Following the football team. Doing a feature on their workout."

"Which magazine?"

"*ManHut.*"

"You are not serious," I laughed. "*ManHut?*"

"Men's lifestyle magazine. Workouts, fashion, sports, all that."

"Sounds like gay porn."

"I got a whole social media platform. Twitter, Instagram, the shizzle."

"No one says 'shizzle' no more."

"I'ma be on TV," he said.

"You got shot?"

"Don't even play. My own show," Jackson said, smiling. "Reality TV."

"You gonna put them photos on your reality TV show?"

Jackson's face changed. The grin left his eyes and every crease and wrinkle deepened until absence defined his face more than light and color. He spoke from a deep place. "I don't even know what to say about that. You know what though? That was a slave ship." His voice lowered. "A *slave ship*. Don't even ask me how I know. And I ain't one of those back-to-Africa everything-started-with-slavery brothers, but I know I saw a slave ship."

"It's like remembering something you never saw."

"Exactly." His eyes looked far inward, at memories he never shared but I knew anyway. Stories passed down through our families. Silence. Resistance coded in hymns. The humiliating social studies unit on slavery, the Confederate flag bumper stickers sparking a deep rage. "They coming to get us," he said.

"Coming to get who?" I asked.

"Us. All of us. Black people."

"I ain't getting on a ship."

"No, it's a good thing."

"What are you talking about?"

For the first time I could remember, maybe the first time ever, Jackson looked at me, not my legs, my hair, my clothes, or my breasts. Me. The mask of darkness grew and overtook us, blotting out every other sensation except love. Jackson loved me. He always had and he always would. It wasn't a crush or even sexual. He slipped past my defenses and took a long look at my soul. I felt completely exposed, as if he knew every secret thing I buried deep down. If he'd asked, I would have told him not to bother. Nothing down there mattered.

Without speaking, without asking, Jackson took my hand. He unwrapped the gauze bandage. I let him. He exposed my hand and looked at it closely. It looked normal, just like it had in the bathroom at work, no scars or marks. I felt the scars though, under my skin. I knew exactly where they were. I could have closed my eyes and drawn them perfectly.

So did Jackson. He traced his fingers across my palm, right along the X under my skin. The sensation felt intense, like pain but more than pain, or a good pain, a tickle, an electric current set on fire.

What just happened?

After a time, Jackson took a long breath and wrapped my hand again. "You should see Granny Mary," he said. "She might sort you out."

"Who's Granny Mary?"

"She took me and moms in when I was a baby. I just started calling her Granny Mary. She lives right around here."

"Your grandma lives around here? You're from here?"

"Kinda. My family is from a little town called Okahika. Got wiped out a long time ago, but it used to be right there," he said, pointing down the street to the vacant lot. "Now they call it The Through."

"Okahika? My granmé lived in a town called Okahika. Louisiana though, not here."

"There's more than one," he said. "Kinda. It's hard to explain. Where's Ben? I'll ask him to go check on Granny Mary. But you should go too. She'll sort you out. She sorts everybody out."

"Alright, who in the hell are you and what have you done with Jackson?" I said, reaching for his arm so we could stay connected a little longer. "We've been talking and you ain't hit on me once, then you start popping all this deep shit." And you want to pray at my feet. You took my hand. You love me.

I suddenly imagined life with Jackson instead of Ben. I imagined living with a man who saw me, not my clothes, my hair, my body, not the fantasy woman, not who I could be if I only got over this or that. I saw us talk without words, I saw us make love, I saw us falling asleep with our children between us. I saw me set my defenses down. I saw me letting me love him. I saw myself live.

The world slowed down. Jackson leaned over. I looked up at his face, his chin, his lips, and kissed him. I caressed his shoulders, his chest, and traced the muscles along his torso. I reached down between his legs. I wanted to wrap myself around him until he went limp, cried, begged for mercy, until he called me a goddess on his knees and meant it.

A bird cried CHEEPER-CHEEPER TAPE! CHEEPER-CHEEPER-CHEEPER TAPE! Cicadas sang again, and the whole world restarted. We pulled ourselves apart. The sun hung low behind the trees. Clouds skittered by. Free Cookie appeared and curled herself around my legs. And behind her came my boyfriend, Ben.

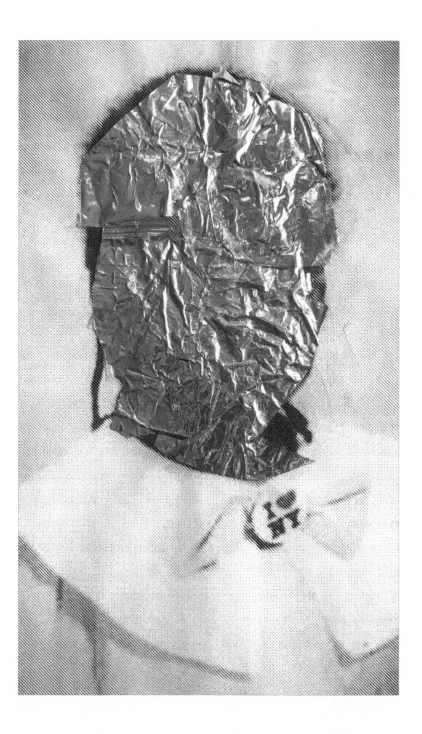

BEN

The Bottletree House

I can't balance. The ship pulled my center of gravity to one side, or the world pulled its own center of gravity to one side. I look down and see that I'm walking. My feet touch the ground. But I list to one side, I think. I can't be sure I'm walking in a straight line, so I just follow Free Cookie home. The Through looks the same: old tires, weeds, broken concrete. I look back, and the ship hovers just past the fence. She looks the same too.

Free Cookie doesn't walk in a straight line. She darts left and right, so I move left and right with her. I'm not exactly quick on my feet today. Free Cookie pees. Now I have to pee. Water drips off my shirt. Free Cookie sniffs around an old tree stump, completely unconcerned with flying ships or my pee. She hears something. Her ears twitch and she looks away without blinking. Then she sprints off towards home. I do my best to keep up.

Adrian stands in the driveway, next to a man I almost recognize. He looks familiar. He's tall, good looking. I've seen him recently. They don't see me yet. They pull apart like they had been hugging. Adrian touches his arm like they're old lovers. I'm not a jealous man. Any two people who want to be together should be together by choice, not because they swore some vows or some ancient code of loyalty. But tonight, tonight I want Adrian to myself. I need her. I need to talk to her, to tell her what happened. She might think I'm crazy. Maybe I am crazy. Maybe I should just keep all this to myself.

But the ship, I could say. Just walk down there with me and you'll see it too.

Unless it's not there anymore. Unless the ship moved. Or it was never really there. Ships can't fly, they can't, it's impossible.

I see *Yemaya* over and over. *Yemaya* spears me through the heart. I can't stop seeing her.

"Cookie!" Adrian squeals. She bends down and scoops Free Cookie into her arms. "Ben, you found her."

"Found. Yes." I say. "Found."

"Yo," the man says, "What's Gucci, my nigga?" Confident, secure voice. My friend from undergrad. The only other black writer in my grad program. A man who writes about push-ups and leg curls and poses on top of models on top of bearskin rugs.

"Ethiopia Jackson," I say. "How you doing?"

"To the east my brother, to the east."

Adrian laughs, "Jackson came to visit his grandmother."

"Yeah," he says. "Well, no. I'm traveling with the football team. Doing a spread on their calf-strengthening regimen for the magazine. Cut Calves by Christmas."

"Right," I try to joke, "Like that arm workout thing you did." I look at the trees across the street. Did something move? Wind. It's just wind.

"You saw it?" he says and smiles. "One of my best."

"Is that what you do with your degree?" I ask. "Write workout lists for men's magazines?"

"Nonfiction's where the money's at," he says. "I'm pulling low six figures right now, but my agent thinks I'll have a reality show by next year."

I cannot believe what I'm hearing. "Reality show?"

"What?"

"On television?"

"What?"

"You're getting a TV show?"

"OKAY!" Jackson yells.

Adrian and Jackson burst into laughter. I feel stupid. Just then, I realize how absurd I must look: teetering over, soaked to the skin, eyes wide, teeth on edge, hand desperately holding my chest, twitchy. Of course they're laughing at me. I look over my shoulder. Nothing's there. Althea said *Yemaya* wouldn't go past the fence right now. Now doesn't mean never. We need to get in the house before it does. I don't have time for old jokes. And I really have to pee.

"Jackson," Adrian says, "can you stay for dinner?"

He flashes his huge smile. "My beautiful goddess, wish I could, but I'm meeting the team at the airport. That's why I came by. I need a favor."

A favor? "A favor?" I ask.

"Thanks man. Knew I could count on you. See, Moms sent me to lay eyes on Granny Mary. I dropped by but she wasn't home. So go over and take a picture of her, then text it to me and I'll text it to Moms and we all straight."

No, I think. No, I'm sure your mother wants you to, I don't know, have a conversation with your own grandmother. Ask how she's doing, how's her health, does anything need doing. And then she'll want you to sit and hear some old story and eat five tons of food. And if we go, she will know we live in the area and invite us to come back and I'll feel too guilty not to sit and eat pickled pig's feet or grits or some southern delicacy while she tells me about her successful and perfect grandson. A flying ship killed me, should have killed me. No.

"Of course we will," Adrian says.

"Nefertiti on the Nile." He plants an exaggerated kiss on her cheek. "You da bomb."

Free Cookie starts squirming in Adrian's arms.

"No one says 'da bomb' anymore," Adrian says.

"I'm bringing it back," Jackson replies.

"Maybe we should get Cookie inside," I say. "She's been gone for a few days."

"Y'all can walk to her place," Jackson says. He points down the street and starts talking. I move and look the way he's pointing. My brain slows into stillness. Ethiopia Jackson is sending us back into The Through. My heart pounds so hard I can hear it. I grind my teeth to keep them from chattering.

"Go on to The Through." He knows The Through. Of course he knows. "Take a right." He waves his fingers. "And follow until you get to the end. You'll see her house. Little place, big garden, blue windows. And you kinda have to go now. Past sundown, she won't answer the door."

"She gardens?" Adrian asks. Free Cookie jumps down. "Ben, you should ask her about your tree."

"You planted this?" Jackson asks. He pats the crown of the peach tree affectionately, like a sickly child. "Your tree needs Viagra."

"Yeah," I say. "Do you have her address? We can GPS it and drive."

"Oh no," Jackson says, "GPS won't work over there. No real street anyway."

"Ben, it's a perfect afternoon for a walk," Adrian says.

"Perfect," I say.

Jackson says whatever he says next, shakes my hand, hugs and kisses Adrian again, calls her a goddess again, mounts his motorcycle and roars off.

Free Cookie meows at us. Adrian lets her inside.

"Okay, let's go," Adrian says.

I look at my shirt. "I got wet looking for Cookie. I should clean up."

"You look like you always look," she says.

I lean in to give her a hug. Adrian puts her hand on my chest and says, "Don't get me wet."

We walk together without touching, back the way I came, back into the Through. I should warn Adrian about the ship. She would never believe me. I don't believe me.

Yemaya spears me through the heart.

The sun hangs low in the trees. The cicadas have begun winding the world again, like today is a day like any other day, like nothing unusual happened today, like they can say 'hey Ben, you don't look so good, why don't you chill out and take a nap?'

I don't like falling asleep, I'd reply. Sleeping is just fine. Falling asleep is creepy. Falling asleep feels like a slow decline into nothingness. I feel myself ebbing away, bit by bit, like a sand castle abandoned to fate by its maker who never gave a shit that the sand was perfectly happy being sand before he came along and forced it into drawbridges, moats, turrets, walls, chambers with little princesses tormented by gnomes. Who thinks of gnomes? Why *falling* asleep? When I fall, I land on something and it hurts. I've fallen and bumped my knee, my elbow, and felt sharp pain shoot to all sorts of places that had nothing to do with the part that fell. Innocent bystanders, so to speak. Come to think of it, the part that gets hurt isn't the part that falls. It's not at fault. It's not as if I'm walking along on the sidewalk and my elbow trips on a crack in the sidewalk. It's not as if I'm skipping through a meadow on a sunny day, where wildflowers bloom and bunnies hump and then my knee gets caught on a rock. But the knee, the elbow, the wrist takes the impact, so I suppose it's justified making all the other parts wake up and recognize how monumentally wrong this falling idea is.

When I do finally fall asleep, there's always this moment when I see seagulls and cough. Some sinus issue I should get checked. I sip some water and settle back down. My throat feels raw, and I hear a tiny rattle in my chest. I think I'm getting sick, but I'm not. I almost never get sick. In fact, I'm totally boring that way. Adrian said once, "You're totally boring." She meant it well. I have no crisis in my life, not until today anyway. I'm relatively healthy for a man my age. No chronic illnesses, no smoker's cough or high blood pressure to watch out for. I broke a few bones as a child, but they all healed cleanly and don't ache. All my moving parts still move. I get a flu shot every year, and then get the flu anyway, but they say that its less severe if you get the shot, so I suppose that's good. I eat right, exercise, and usually maintain a good erection when we have sex. Which was not last night. Or the night before that.

Judging by the way her shoulders square off, we won't have sex tonight either. Adrian walks quickly and I have to hurry to keep up. My legs feel heavy and slow.

But I'm a crisis-free type of guy. A save-the-drama-for-Obama type of guy. When bad stuff happens, I just let it pass on through. I absorb what happens, but don't hold on forever. Maybe that's why certain women—the jogger, Adrian, Althea—feel drawn to me. I'm porous. Here, they say, here's all my messy bits. I've been looking for just the right guy to clean this up. Ben, Ben, Ben, they say, how much can you soak up?

A lot, I bet.

Let's see how much. No, don't go to sleep, they say. And don't roll over and try to poke Adrian into having sex. That never works.

Why doesn't it work?

Because, they say, exasperated.

Adrian clicks her low heels on the pavement as we pass from the faux-historic district into the place I just left. Even though I'm flushed and sweaty, walking next to my girlfriend who still smells faintly of the perfume she wears to work, I smell deep ocean. I inhale and take that long breath you only take in the presence of the sea.

When I was a kid, we moved to a small town called New City because the founders couldn't think of a better name. New City might have been the most boring place on the planet. And six months later, we moved away. I don't remember much about the town except the seagulls. We lived a good 35 miles from the sea, but seagulls converged daily in a shopping center parking lot. We used to shop there, at the A&P and a few other stores. I remember a bagel place, and a pizza place, but that was the 80's. Every corner had a bagel place and a pizza place. That's not remarkable. But I remember seagulls wafting above the parking lot, crying. Sometimes they landed and dug through trash. Sometimes they just walked around. I could never figure out why seagulls would land so far from home.

I don't know why I'm thinking of them just now. It's not like I suddenly heard a seagull and triggered a memory. But, I'd tell the cicadas, I see seagulls as I sleep.

We enter the Through, but instead of going left, downstream, towards the fence and *Yemaya* we turn right, upstream. This part has less junk and more tall weeds. I should tell Adrian about what happened. She'll never believe me. I should tell her. *Yemaya* speared me through the heart. Just like that. I can't. Say it.

After about ten minutes, Adrian stumbles in some unseen hole. I reach out for her and notice a gauze bandage wrapped around her left hand. The bandage looks thicker over her palm. Had that been there before? It wasn't there this morning, I don't think.

"Thanks," she says. "I should have worn better shoes."

"What happened to your hand?" I ask.

"Oh that." Adrian pulls her hand away. "It's nothing. A scratch. I picked up some stuff for it at the pharmacy before I came home."

"Looks big for a scratch," I say.

"Stop worrying," she says. Adrian points at a little patch of woods. "Is that the house?"

At first, I don't see anything but scrubby trees. As we get closer, I begin to see the outlines of a clearing, and a little path we could have followed if we'd come from the other direction. Adrian steadies herself on small trees and I try not to get stuck in the mud. The house has no fence, but Jackson's grandmother keeps a large garden full of all sorts of plants in a clearing. I can't help but sense that all of these plants live here for a reason, that Jackson's grandmother placed each plant in a particular spot and nowhere else. She's clearly skilled at gardening. I really should ask her about my peach tree.

The house itself looks like any old person's house I suppose. Low, with a wooden ramp built so she wouldn't have to take the steps. White window boxes with flowers. A huge, rusty mailbox near the entrance to the path that doesn't look like it's been used in a long time. A name scrawled on the mailbox reads 'C Mary'. Large blue glass windows. This is no cheap film covering or even stained glass. This is blue cobalt glass like I've seen in antique stores, depression glass, so dark it reflects a blue haze over the window boxes.

"God, Ben," Adrian says. "It looks like a bottletree."

"What's a bottletree?" I ask.

"You never heard of a bottletree?" Adrian shakes her head slightly. "People make bottletree sculptures these days.

Remember that house up the street from us, with the metal sculpture and the bottles?"

"Oh sure," I lie. "I think so."

"That's bottletree art," she says. "No one would want the real thing in their yard. It's too creepy."

"What's the real thing?"

"When I was a kid," she starts. Adrian never, never talks about her childhood. "We had real bottletrees. Not in town, where I lived, but out in the country. Way, way out. We'd visit my grandparents on the farm, and me and my sister would sneak me out to see the real thing. Kids weren't supposed to get near it."

"Why?" I ask. "It's just a tree, right?"

"Sorta. See, people would find a young tree and push bottles into the branches. Into the crooks of branches, or just make a hole on one side and push the bottle in. The tree would grow over the bottle. They always used blue glass bottles, that's why I thought of it."

"People did that? Why?"

"Well, my sister told me that if a witch walked by, the bottletree would suck out her soul and trap her forever. We used to dare each other to touch one."

"Did you?"

"No, I was always too scared." She laughed a little.

Every now and then, Adrian mentions her sister. Never by name, just 'my sister.' If I press or ask too many questions, Adrian stops talking, or changes the subject, or picks a fight. I've learned to leave it alone.

"So, I guess we should knock?" I ask.

"I suppose so," Adrian says.

Neither of us moves.

"Just go knock," Adrian says.

"Okay." I take a deep breath. The salt air smell is long gone, replaced by the strong plants growing in this garden. "Okay." I walk up the little ramp to the door. As I do, I realize the dark blue windows could easily hide Jackson's grandmother from us. She could have been watching us the whole time.

I raise my hand to knock. Shit, shit. "Adrian!" I say in a loud stage whisper.

"What?" she replies.

"What do I call her? Jackson's grandmother?"

"He said Granny Mary."

"I can't call her Granny."

"Well, his last name is Jackson. Mother Jackson."

"Okay, okay." I raise my hand, and the door knocks. The door knocks on its own. I'm standing there, with my fist up in the air like a Black Panther, and the door knocks of its own accord. I look at Adrian. She looks at me. The door knocks a second time. I put my hand on the doorknob. Just then, I see that the hinges face the wrong way. This wrong-way door will open towards me, not into the house. The doorknob though, feels solid in my hand, real. Relax, I tell myself. This is just an eccentric old lady who lives in an odd house and gardens. She probably has some dementia. That's why Jackson didn't want to come out here. He so owes me.

The door knocks a third time. I turn the handle. The door opens easily, and Jackson's grandmother stands in the door, looking as solid and non-demented and un-eccentric as possible.

"Hello children," she said in a deep voice. "Care for some scotch?"

Adrian and I sat on a hard couch covered in plastic while Jackson's grandmother got glasses and ice in the kitchen. The 'front room' as she called it, had nothing I expected, no quilts, knickknacks, or old photos. Instead, I felt like I'd entered an art gallery. Every piece of furniture featured some handmade decoration, and I suspected that Jackson's grandmother had done all of the work. She had covered the low wooden coffee table in front of us with plant diagrams. Each leaf, flower, root and stem had been carefully drawn or painted, then elegantly labelled. Adrian traced the drawings with her hands. She had such exquisite hands. Hen Weed, Aloe Vera, Baobab, Lavender, Rose, Queen Elizabeth Root, Agrimony, a few others. As I read the last name, Adrian traced the same plant - Althea - and we both jumped like we'd been shocked.

Jackson's grandmother came out with a tray, three glasses with ice, and a dusty bottle. "You like my pictures?" she asked.

"You painted these?" Adrian asked.

"Don't sound so shocked," she said. "I used to work with herbs and roots. Now I mostly garden and paint a little. My hands and eyes still work, but I shot my knees to shit looking for that one." She nodded towards a large daisy growing in a clear glass jar. "Took me years to find her."

"Mother Jackson," Adrian said, "Why did you look for that flower? Will the roots do something special? Is that why you put it in glass?"

"Mother Jackson! Who the fuck told you to call me Mother Jackson? Y'all call me Cut Mary."

In unison we said, "Yes, Mrs. Cut Mary."

"I ain't no missus," she said and smiled. "All these years, never been married. Got some of the best dick on the planet though, believe that."

"Um," I said. "Yes. Cut Mary."

"Did I scandalize you?" she asked. Yes, I wanted to say. My whole day has been one woman after another acting strangely. The jogger, Althea, even Adrian. *Yemaya* speared me through the heart.

Instead of speaking, I just closed my mouth.

"Good," Cut Mary said. "You look like you need some scandal. As for that daisy, she's a whole nother story. But I feel like y'all came here for a reason."

"Yes," I said. "Your grandson sent us. He asked us to check on you."

"And send him a picture," Adrian added.

"Right," I said. "A picture."

"Picture of what?" Cut Mary asked.

"You. He asked for a picture of you."

"A picture of me? Who sent you?" Cut Mary demanded.

"Jackson. Ethiopia Jackson," I said. "Your grandson. We went to college together."

"Never had a baby," Cut Mary said.

No babies? So no grandkids? Oh shit. What if we came to the wrong house? What if there's another garden house with blue windows just past here and Jackson's poor frail granny is laying in a ditch? Okay, that's not realistic.

I'm sitting in a bottletree house talking to Jackson's grandmother about her sex life. I am no judge of realistic.

"Alright, alright. Let me sort this out," Cut Mary said. "You say this man say he my grandson and asked y'all to come check on me. Ethiopia Jackson."

"Yes ma'am."

"Well, I never had a natural child, and even if I did her children and their children would be long dead by now." Cut Mary mumbled something I couldn't make out. "I have taken in a few, from time to time. Some of them call me mama. What he look like?"

"Tall," I said.

"Very handsome," Adrian said. "Straight teeth, dimples, perfect smooth skin. All kinds of muscles."

Oh really.

"Uh-huh. But not the smartest boy you ever met?" Cut Mary asked.

"Yeah. No," Adrian conceded.

"Hm. I took in a girl years ago with a baby named Ethiopia. Raised right here. Ain't seen them in a long time."

I had questions, like how I'd known Jackson since the 90's and he never mentioned where he grew up. But we'd stepped into someone else's family drama. I wanted to leave. "We didn't mean to bother you," I said. "If we could just take a quick photo?"

"Light ain't much, but go ahead, young man, go ahead."

I took out my phone and pressed the button. Nothing happened. I pressed it over and over. Still nothing.

"Hurt your hand honey?" Cut Mary asked Adrian.

Adrian folded her hand. "It's nothing," she said. "I scratched it."

"I have no power," I said. Weird. I charged my phone every night. The battery normally lasted a full day.

"Ben," Adrian sighed, "Just use mine." She pulled her phone out of her purse, but it didn't work either. "Huh," she said. "I'm dead."

"No juice?" Cut Mary said. "Well now. We gonna hafta fix that." Cut Mary drained her glass and walked into another room, slowly. Her knees must have ached. I wondered why her family didn't have her knees fixed, but old people get stubborn. She may have refused to go.

"Do you think she has a charger?" Adrian asked.

"Doesn't seem like the smart phone type," I said. In fact, I couldn't remember electric lines running to the house at all. I looked at the walls. Cut Mary had no lamps, sockets, outlets, or any electrical devices of any kind, at least nothing I could see from the couch. I looked by the wrong-way door for a light switch. It didn't have a light switch. The last sunlight shone through the blue windows, giving the house the look of deep, deep water.

"Yeah," Adrian agreed.

We didn't say anything for a bit.

"So," Adrian said, "How was your day? Anything interesting happen? And where did you find Free Cookie?"

How *was* my day?

Anything *interesting* happen?

Where *did* I find Free Cookie?

I wanted to confess everything right then and there: the jogger, the attractive old woman, the ship crashing through the trees, The Through, but when I opened my mouth I felt an urge to cry. *Yemaya* speared me through the heart. I took a long, shuddering breath. "We should think about leaving soon," I said. "We can't get the photo, and she seems fine."

"So strange," Adrian said.

"What's strange?"

"I mean, she seems capable and all, but living out here alone? With her plants and her bad knees?"

"Cut Mary? Yeah, she's an odd one."

"I don't know. She seems happy."

"Besides, we should re-wrap your scratch. The bandage probably got dirty on our way here."

Adrian turned and looked at me squarely. "Ben, you went to church as a kid."

I nodded. "A zillion churches, sure."

140

"Did they ever talk about the saints? St. Peter, St. Jaques, any of them?"

I should add religion to the list of things Adrian never talked about. At least I understood. She was raised Louisiana Catholic, but became an atheist after Katrina. I emerged soaking wet from the Hudson River and became an atheist. Whatever answers existed for us, religion didn't have them.

"Never," I said. "No saints in Baptist churches."

"My family had two religions. Well, one religion with two versions: city and country. The city version was basically Catholicism, although our music was way better."

"You're from New Orleans," I said. "Of course the music is better."

Adrian smiled. "Out in the country, it's not like they didn't go to church. They did. But they believed in other stuff. Spirits, haints, root medicine."

"Sounds like voodoo," I said.

"No one ever said it out loud," Adrian said. "But yeah, that's probably the best word for it."

"Holy shit, really?" I said. "Like voodoo dolls and all that?"

"The dolls are fakes."

"What? No way."

"Fake."

"But—"

"Most of what people think of voodoo is completely fake," Adrian said.

"I mean, I know you and I don't believe in religion, but some people get something from it."

"That's not what I mean," Adrian said. "The way they explained it, the real thing, voodoo or vodun or whatever you call it, is dangerous. Terrifying. And it's not about right and wrong so much as power. Some gods have power in certain situations, and others have power over objects or elements."

"So they pray to the god who can do what they need?"

"Pray, sing, worship, sure. But that's only one direction."

"Direction?"

"It works both ways. We can ask things from them and they can ask things of us." When I didn't reply, she said, "Possession. I only saw it once. But anyway, the dolls and all that crap let people think they're doing voodoo when they're not. So in a way, they do have a function. They protect people who aren't ready for the actual thing, and let true believers worship in private."

"I get it." I didn't get it, but I'd sort it out later. The important thing was to keep Adrian talking. "Um, what about the zombies?"

"Oh that's fucked up. I don't even like to think about that."

"Like The Walking Dead?"

"Shows don't even come close. They're like the dolls, meaningless. Meaningless for voodoo. During slavery, slave masters took everything they could. Labor, sex, possessions, music, anything of value. But they could never take a soul. So as long as people had their souls, they were never really slaves."

"Sure, okay, makes sense."

Adrian dropped her voice low. "This is fucked up. If a slave violated the slave community, like murder or rape, something serious, then the slave community punished them. A voodoo priest asked the gods to remove the offender's soul. Without a soul, he turned into a real slave - no willpower, no dreams, no desires, just endless work."

I'd never heard of anything so horrible. "It's a metaphor, right? A mode of thinking? A way slaves understood their situation? Souls can't be removed, can they?"

Adrian shook her head. "I don't know, Ben. I don't know."

The light faded. Cut Mary's white furniture blended into the shadows, as if we'd entered a realm of eternal night where magical creatures fashioned chairs from passing clouds. After this day, anything seemed possible.

I cracked my knuckles, stretched my hands, and laid them back on the couch. I reached one finger towards Adrian's fingers. Adrian hated public affection or lovey-dovey gestures. So, I pretended that my finger had just settled down next to her finger and our fingers were just friends who could touch casually if they wanted, or not, but it was no big deal either way. Adrian curled her finger around mine. I felt safer when she did that.

"Children," Cut Mary said. I'd missed her return in the darkness. "Easy to get crossed up here. I suppose we should get you fixed." Cut Mary set another tray holding tall glass candles and matches onto the table. "Light those," she said. "I can't find my glasses in all this."

Adrian lit a match, then held the candle sideways to light it. She handed the matches to me, and I lit another. The wicks burst into flame immediately and pushed the darkness back to the blue windows. Couches and tables became real furniture again, and I saw Adrian's profile. I hadn't realized how desperate I was for light. I wanted to hug Adrian right then and there, tell her I loved her, weep, kiss her neck, carry her home in my arms. The candle grew hot. I hadn't realized I was still holding it. "Ow," I said, and set it down.

"Glasses on my head the whole time," Cut Mary said. "Whatever happens, don't get old." She laughed and sat down. "Now let's see what we have." Cut Mary touched the table with the plant designs. "Althea," she said.

Adrian's eyes widened and she sat straight up. She'd placed her candle on the drawing of the Althea plant. Same name as the attractive old woman in The Through.

Cut Mary traced her hands across the painted plant, root, stem, leaf, and flower. "The roots attract good spirits and help you find what you're looking for. Leaves attract good spirits, increase spiritual power, heal, soothe. Also known as Rose of Sharon." Cut Mary pushed her glasses back and took a hard look at Adrian. "I can see how you need something like that."

"I didn't, I don't," Adrian stammered. "I just set the candle down on the table."

"You could have set that candle anywhere, but you didn't," Cut Mary said. You put it where you needed it honey, where it needed to be. But you knew that."

Neither of us said anything. I heard my heartbeat, low, soft, unsteady.

"Is the past real and solid and physical, or just stories we tell each other?" Cut Mary asked. "If you could go back in time, could you fix your mistakes? Could you put that candle somewhere else? Is the past done when it's done or still going? Does the past move?" She sighed and leaned back into the armchair.

I tried to think of an answer. Does the past move? The question seemed ridiculous. The past can't move, it's done, we're done. When Captain Sisko dreamed of being a black sci-fi writer in the Fifties, his dreams didn't change the present.

Unless they did.

"I can't answer your question," Cut Mary said.

What question?

"But," Cut Mary continued, looking straight at Adrian. "I can say what you won't."

I turned and looked at Adrian. My neck felt stiff. I'd held it in one position for too long. Adrian pressed her long fingers to her mouth. Her jaw twitched, and her eyes swelled. I realized Adrian might cry in front of me. I'd never seen her cry, ever. When she cried, if she cried, she cried alone.

"Althea. Althea was my mother's name." Adrian said quietly.

Adrian and I met just before Katrina, but I never met her family. After the disaster, we lost touch for a few years. Then

I heard from her out of the blue. She asked if I still cared about her and could she stay with me temporarily, until she sorted things out. I said yes. Adrian arrived with the clothes on her back and a Red Cross bag of toiletries, like the flood had happened a week ago, not years before. She had no family photos, no documents, nothing. It took us years to get her a driver's license, as we couldn't find a birth certificate or any official thing that said Adrian Dussett.

Adrian had never mentioned her mother's name or told me anything about her. I'd always wanted to know more. Now that I did, I felt ashamed. I wanted to go back and undo every time I asked about her mother and every time Adrian changed the subject or refused to answer. But I couldn't. All I could do was hold her awkwardly. Adrian took a huge breath, then began crying. She rocked back and forth.

Cut Mary produced a box of tissues (doesn't every old woman have a box of tissues handy?) and said, "Let it out baby. Let it out."

"She floated away in the flood," Adrian said, gulping air between sobs. "I should - have rescued - her but - I didn't. She died – I let her - my fault. Mama, my uncle - my fault - my fault, my fault."

I didn't know what to do. I looked at Cut Mary.

She said, "I'll fix y'all some more drink."

I nodded like 'drink' was a sensible suggestion.

"People go when it's time to go," Cut Mary said. "No sooner, no later."

"It wasn't her time," Adrian said.

"Set the candle here and see something. Set the candle there and see something else," Cut Mary said as she poured us another pair of scotches.

Adrian downed hers in one gulp, bumped, and cried again. I held her, but that seemed as real as a voodoo doll.

"Ben, seems like you need help too. Now are you gonna tell me, or do I have to guess?"

"Guess?"

"Why you smell like seawater."

Adrian looked at me sharply.

"Does my candle signify anything?" I asked. In the dark, I'd placed it over a low plant with broad leaves and purple flowers hanging down.

"Comfrey," Cut Mary said. "Planning a trip?"

"No, I don't think so," I said.

"On a flying ship?"

I stood straight up like I'd been jolted with electricity. "*Yemaya*? You're that old woman I met today in The Through. You've been screwing with me all day."

"You saw the ship?" Adrian asked.

"Your name's Althea, not Cut Mary, you just look different now," I said. "And you, you, you…" Found me. Rescued me. Pushed the ship back with your hands. Led me out.

"Ben, let me tell you something serious." Cut Mary looked at me. "I haven't left this house for years and years. Years and years and years. You didn't meet me in The Through, although the fact that you met anyone at all is something. And you saw the ship. Your problems have just started."

Cut Mary yawned. I suddenly felt sleepy. Adrian yawned.

"But this is more than one old woman can handle all in one night. Take these," she said. Cut Mary handed us cuttings of althea and comfrey wrapped in a thin paper bag marked with an exaggerated red X on one side, like a pirate map.

"Plant them when you get home," Cut Mary instructed. "Come back tomorrow, and I'll tell you the rest. Oh and by the way, Adrian, I got you a little present. He's outside."

Adrian and I looked at each other. He?

"Take him home, tell him what to do," Cut Mary continued. "He'll do whatever you want. Now give me a hug, I'm a hugger." She embraced us both, and then the door opened and we stood outside on the little wheelchair ramp again.

From the ramp, we saw a barrel-chested man hunched over the mailbox. His skin might have been dark brown once, but some illness had changed him into a motley, brown with white and black patches across his face, arms and hands. His hair had grown out long and begun to form dreadlocks at the ends. His beard had also grown long and shaggy. He looked tall, perhaps six-four or six-five. Dirt crusted his huge, thick-fingered hands. In fact, filth clung to his entire body. His clothes and hair looked like he'd jumped in a swamp and taken a nap.

Cut Mary popped her head out of the door. "Hey," she said, "get on over here. You belong to Adrian now."

The man turned and walked towards us in a slow shuffle, head held down.

"He's all yours dear," Cut Mary said. "Don't worry about feeding him. Marcel don't eat."

Adrian gripped my arm I thought she would break it. "Marcel? Cut Mary, what—"

Cut Mary shut the door. Marcel walks to the edge of the stairs and stops.

"What are we supposed to do?" I ask. Adrian doesn't reply, but her heart pounds so hard I can feel her pulse in her fingers.

Marcel stinks like rotting roadkill. He must bathe in the stagnant water along the river's edge. "Ugh, disgusting," I say. "Well, we can hose him off at home. There must be someone we can call, social services."

Adrian still says nothing. Her breath comes in little gasps.

"Babe, are you alright?" I ask.

Adrian shakes her head. I can't tell if she means yes or no. I decide going home is the best thing for all of us.

"Sir," I say in an overloud voice, "we're going. We'll get you cleaned up and see if there's someone we can call for you."

Marcel doesn't move. In fact, he hasn't moved since he reached the porch. He still holds his head down and hunches his back. His hands hang loosely at his sides.

Adrian looks sharply at Marcel. Then she walks up to him and takes his chin in her hand. She pushes his face up and looks at him closely.

"Sir?" I call again. "Sir? Mister Marcel?" Students occasionally call me 'Mr. Ben', which I always correct to Professor Hughes or just Professor. I know that's a southern tradition, but it annoys me. Maybe it annoys him too.

Adrian shrieks, drops his face, and runs back to Cut Mary's door. She pounds on the door, "Cut Mary! What the fuck? Cut Mary!"

"Whoa, whoa," I say, grabbing her hands. Adrian pants like a wild thing, eyes wide and teeth bared.

"Get off me!" Adrian screams, shaking herself loose.

"What's wrong with you?"

Adrian pounds the door again. "Cut Mary! Cut Mary!"

"Adrian!" I yell, grabbing her hands again.

Adrian rips her hands away from me. Her face contorts, as if every emotion inside her fights for control. I'm about to ask again what's going on when Adrian reaches back, balls up her fist, and punches me in the eye.

"Holy shit!" One eye swells shut, while the other wells with tears. I can barely see. My ears increase their volume in response. I hear Adrian fly off the porch and attack Marcel, slapping, hitting, kicking him, screaming, "You're dead! You're dead! I saw you! Fuck you Marcel, fuck you! Fuck you!"

Dimly, I see Marcel stand there and take Adrian's beating. He doesn't move or defend himself in any way, and shows no pain at all.

Adrian howls at him, a long, guttural, aching sound. Then she falls to her knees and cries. I go to her and hold her, gently this time. I know that sounds ridiculous. "Ben," she says, "Meet my Uncle Marcel. He died in Katrina."

My watery eye flattens the distance between me and Marcel and Adrian. We sit uncomfortably close, Picasso figures, one hunched and silent, one weeping, one pained; three sides of one anguish. The light settles over the house, darkening the windows and sending the flowers to sleep. Adrian and I knock on Cut Mary's door to ask her to fix this, to undo whatever she's done, but her door refuses to open again.

B E N

Hoppin' John

The cicadas reset while we sat in Cut Mary's garden house with the blue windows. Now they whir without pause. Marcel follows us, lumbering and silent. The attractive old woman I met in The Through, Althea, could have been Adrian's mother. I want to ask Adrian about her family and what happened to them, but the cicadas have got the world running and my voice might ruin the whole thing. Besides, I don't think she has any more idea than I do.

The new moon rises ahead. The sun is no lower than it was when we arrived. How much time did we spend at Cut Mary's? A week, a day, an hour, a second, a millisecond, flying, motionless, Xeno's arrow eternally suspended in mid-air. A few stars twinkle overhead. From this angle, they look like a cross. A passing cloud looks like a fish.

We walk in our own silences. Adrian hasn't apologized for hitting me and I don't expect she will. I put my arm around

Adrian's waist and she wraps her arm around mine. I admit, normally I would have tried to turn that into some sort of sexual gesture. I don't feel like putting a move on her right now. It's silly that I'm still putting moves on my girlfriend of five years and besides, I'm not in the mood. I'm awake, but tired and sore, my eye hurts, and my shoes squish on every step. I want to go home and tell Adrian everything over dinner. Dinner. I never cooked. Maybe it's good that I never cooked. We'll have to order something. But our phones died in Cut Mary's house. We'll have to eat our phones. An image comes to mind, a line drawing in the New Yorker: me and Adrian, sitting at our little dining table, knife, plate, fork, glass. A cell phone sits on each plate. Her mouth opens. I strain trying to see what she says, but the caption fades away. Maybe I'll ask Adrian later.

That makes no sense. Adrian will tell me that makes no sense. Because that makes no sense.

Ben, I think, you've had a hard day.

Every day, I think, every freaking day.

I am the little man someone draws in the corner of a dull textbook. Flick the pages and my life simulates movement. *Is the past real and solid and physical, or just stories we tell each other?* I can't stop thinking about her question. If the past is stories, can they be rewritten? Can a new narrator take over, retell the same set of events? I once asked my literature students what fiction was. One smart-ass said, "It's fake, duh." I didn't have a smart-ass reply.

My parents always pushed the African heritage stuff on me. They're both regular suburbanites, but Dad says he was a Black Panther back in the day. Or he knew some Black Panthers. Or he saw one once, but whatever, the point is that deep down inside, he has the heart of a revolutionary. Mom always dreamed of this foundation, a non-profit, that sends black kids back to Africa for a few weeks. They always tried to get me interested, but I never listened. Even in college, when it was fashionable to wear Africa-shaped leather medallions, I only went Afrocentric to pick up girls. That never worked. In fact, as I remember, the whole Afrocentric thing got Ethiopia Jackson laid but not me. And then I went to graduate school and found a job and taught and I was just too busy living to think about it.

I'm all over the place today. I need to get out of my head and back to reality. Marcel's shadow falls across our feet. The sun falls below the trees behind us, and a bright new moon rises ahead. Every leaf and branch along the jogging trail casts a long shadow away from the sun, but soon the shadows will switch and move away from the moon. We're close enough to town that people walk their dogs and push kids learning to ride bikes along the jogging trail. We'll be able to see the fence and *Yemaya* before we turn for home.

That's what I'll do. If we get there and we can see the ship, then I'll say, Hey Adrian, what's that?

And she'll say, What's what?

And I'll say, Kinda looks like a ship.

And she'll say, Let's go take a look. Oh by the way, sorry about your eye. And then I can tell her the rest.

We get to the branch in the path. One way takes us home, and the other takes us to *Yemaya*. I look down there. Everything seems normal. No flying ship, no old women. We go home. Marcel tries to follow us inside, but Adrian says "Stop," and he freezes mid-stride on the sidewalk.

Adrian showers while I cook. I turn on NPR.

Terry Gross asks someone how it feels to get a six-figure advance before he writes his first novel.

I turn NPR off.

I pour some oil in the cast-iron skillet and wait for it to heat up. That's important. Hot oil cooks food, but cold oil gets soaked up and makes everything taste greasy. Once the oil heats up, I add two strips of turkey bacon and let them crisp up. While the bacon cooks, I dice onion and garlic. Then I remove the bacon and add the onions. If I add the garlic now, it will burn. I used to burn garlic all the time. Now I wait until the onions turn nearly translucent before adding the garlic. I love the smell of onions and garlic cooking. Maybe that's why I always added the garlic too early, just for the smell. I open a can of purple hull peas, rinse them in cold water, and let them drain. Once most of the water is gone, I stir the peas into the onions and garlic, then add salt and black pepper. These peas need about five minutes. While I'm waiting, I take a bag of pre-washed spinach out of the refrigerator, some leftover rice, a can of cut okra, tomatoes, and squash, and a bottle of hot sauce. Hopping' John. Not exactly from scratch, but tasty and quick. I learned this dish as a teenager, after my mother quit cooking and I had to learn to feed myself.

We had taken her out to dinner somewhere – me and Dad. She had turned 40. We probably took her to one of those restaurants that middle class families liked. Red Lobster, I think. I don't remember the meal at all. On the way home, my mother said, "I have an announcement. I've been cooking for 30 years and I'm done. I'm not cooking another thing, ever." We laughed. Ha ha, a black woman from the South who refuses to cook? That's a sitcom, not real life. You should write for Cosby.

She was serious. The next day, she refused to make breakfast, so I caught the early bus and ate breakfast at school. Lunch too. Then I came home and nothing was ready, so I ordered a pizza. As usual, Dad worked late. The next day happened just the same, and on through Friday. My parents fought all weekend. I took the family car and got takeout from the Korean grocery. The food tasted delicious, unlike anything I'd ever had.

The store owner, Mrs. Hong, saw me come inside the store after school every day, buy a small snack and dinner for one, plus a drink. Then I'd leave without making any small talk. One day, she called out to me.

"Hey there."

She had a thick accent, not a Korean or Asian-y accent but from the Deep South. She sounded like one of my relatives.

"Um, hi."

"You always in here eating for one. Ain't you got no people?"

Something in her voice hit me, just hard enough to resonate. An insistent tap that cracks concrete bit by bit until the prisoner escapes. I never knew if the pitch of her voice did it, or the rhythm, or the softness in her vowels, or the way her mouth crinkled up after she finished speaking, or all of the above. I saw myself at home, eating alone, while Mom watched TV in the bedroom, and Dad worked late again. I saw kids walking to the morning bus, still eating the breakfast their mothers had made, after I'd poured myself another bowl of cereal, eaten it, and put the bowl and spoon in the dishwasher, then left without saying goodbye because the house was already empty. I began to cry, and then cried because I was crying, and then cried because I was ashamed of crying because I was crying.

Mrs. Hong hurried from behind the counter and hugged me. She was short and round-ish, matronly, dressed in an animal print wrap, plus a gold ring on each finger and huge hoop earrings. I was a tall, gangly 16-year-old with a low fade, acne scars, dressed as close to fashionable as I could in 1986— pastel green pants, pink shirt, bolo tie with silver tips. We must have looked ridiculous. And then I told her my whole story, of my mother not cooking, her birthday, dad working, moving around, and how I didn't even know how to boil water. About not having any people. So she put me to work, after school and weekends, prepping cornbread pudding, succotash, and her famous Hoppin' John, then delivering Korean soul food to everyone else eating alone.

Adrian comes out of the shower, patting her hair with a towel. "What a day," she says. "Is there any wine left?"

"I think so. Do you want a glass?"

"Yeah."

We have a bottle of inexpensive champagne in the refrigerator door. Neither of us feel like celebrating, but it would do. I pour Adrian a healthy glass and pour one for myself. Adrian drinks half of her glass in one go without saying a word. I stand next to her, close enough to reach out if she wanted a hug, but not so close that she would feel crowded. This has all happened before. People who don't understand me and Adrian might believe that she's this dynamic, go-getter, A-type personality in public, and a mess at home, where I'm a sort of follower, never ahead of the next wave type of guy, but solid as a rock in our relationship. Truthfully, Adrian is Adrian all the time. She's dynamic and assertive wherever she goes, and I'm under the waves at home or abroad. The talking and crying this afternoon was an aberration. I'd like to think that we can pick who we are in certain times and places, but people just aren't that clear-cut.

Dinner is almost ready. I add the cut okra, tomatoes, and squash, and a few splashes of hot sauce. Once the flavors combine, I'll turn the heat off, crumble up the bacon, and stir in the spinach and bacon until the leaves turn dark green. Mrs. Hong would be proud.

"What the hell is that smell?" Adrian asks.

"It's dinner," I say. "Hoppin' John."

"Smells terrible," she says.

I haven't burnt anything. The recipe came out perfectly, exactly as planned. I don't know what she means. "I don't smell anything wrong," I say.

"You don't smell that?"

"No. I mean I smell the food, but nothing's wrong."

Adrian looks at me like she has never seen anything quite like me before. Not angry, but more puzzled. If I had been a five-legged cow at the state fair, Adrian would have looked at me just like that.

"I can't eat that," she says flatly.

"You've eaten it before," I say.

"I don't care," Adrian replies. "I can't possibly eat that."

I looked at my hands without saying anything.

"Look," she says, "I'll get us some dinner. My treat. What do you want?"

"Whatever you want is fine."

"Oh god, don't be like that," Adrian says.

"Be like what?"

"Forget it."

"Be like what?"

"Just stop it! Okay? Just fucking stop!" Adrian shouts.

"I didn't do anything wrong. I made dinner. A dinner you like," I argue.

"It smells gross."

"Thanks."

"Well it does. What, do you want me to say 'Oh, thanks honey' when you cook something gross? The whole house reeks."

"Fine," I say. "I get it. You don't want this dish ever again." I take the skillet off the stovetop and throw it into the trash.

"What are you doing?" Adrian yells.

"Throwing out food you hate," I yell. "I wanted pizza but I thought after the day we've had a little home cooked meal would be nice. Well fuck me." I don't know why I'm saying this. "I should have kept my stupid ideas to myself."

"You could have eaten it," Adrian says.

"Why don't you punch me again if you hate it so much?" I ask.

Adrian gasps, then runs out of the room. I don't watch where she goes. The front door opens and closes quickly, then I hear the creak of the porch swing. I turn on the radio and listen to NPR again as I finish my champagne. The story is almost over when I tune in. A book review, about some historian who wrote a history of vanished black communities in the South. She's giving a reading on campus tomorrow, the 29th. That date sticks out as if on some great calendar with my whole life stretched out from conception to death and beyond, I'd put 'remember this' on a sticky note and placed it on August 29ᵗʰ. But the sticky note had fallen off. I'd found it stuck to my sock. So I know I should remember something, but I don't know what exactly, or why the 29ᵗʰ sticks out as a day in particular.

I feel like an ass. Adrian finally opens up about her past and I pick a fight with her. Or she picked a fight with me. Smooth move, slick. Maybe it's not all my fault. Maybe we did this together. She's feeling vulnerable and weak, so she lashes out. I am weak, so I lash back. The porch swing creaks again. I can hear her sobbing. I pull the skillet out of the trash, but the food is a total loss. I'm such an idiot. I pour another glass of champagne and take a deep breath. No matter what happened, what I think happened today, I can listen for a bit. I can not be myself for a minute. Whatever happened, I can't figure it out without her.

I take a deep breath, and then another. I'm still off-kilter. The porch swing creaks rhythmically. I try to breathe in time with the swing, but my heart races ahead like a musician who can't keep the beat. Fine, I'll apologize. The bottle has enough to refill Adrian's glass. I grab it and my glass. Did Adrian take her glass with her? Depends, I tell myself, on whether her wineglass is real or just a story.

I open the screen door and find Adrian sitting on the front steps, looking at the night sky. For whatever reason, all the street lights are out tonight. None of the other houses or businesses left their lights on, so the only light comes from our house and the moon. Marcel still stands on the sidewalk, exactly where we left him, one raised leg about to take a step.

Adrian's pulled her knees to her chest and wrapped her arms around them. I sit down next to Adrian and refill her glass, then stretch my legs out and lean back. Cut Mary's plants sit next to some old pots filled with dirt. I'd forgotten all about the plants. I guess Adrian started to plant them and quit. I'll plant them later. A breeze pushes the porch swing back and forth. Cicadas keep ticking along, running the clock of the world without thinking about us one way or another.

"Sorry," she says.

"Sorry," I say.

"I'm really sorry," she says.

"I am too," I say.

We don't say anything for awhile.

"You never talk about your family," I say.

"You don't either," she says.

I don't say anything in particular.

"Families are hard," I say. "You don't have to talk about yours."

"Yes," she says and looks at me. "Yes, I do." Then she turns away and sips her champagne.

The creaking plays counterpoint to the cicadas.

"I don't know how to tell you this," she says. "It's not something I talk about."

"Okay," I say, because I don't know what else to say.

"When I was ten," she says, "I was in back of our house, playing with dolls."

"In New Orleans?" I ask.

"Yeah," Adrian says. "It was late in the day. My uncle." Adrian drinks again. "Him." She points at Marcel. "Saw me playing. Uncle Marcel, he…" Adrian shudders. She begins to sweat. Her breathing gets fast and jerky. I reach my hand towards her but she pushes away. "I'm cold, I'm cold, I'm cold," she repeats, then starts rocking back and forth. "He's not my blood uncle, said that made it okay. He was just a friend of Mama's." She shakes. "He did what he did and I left. It hurt so bad I left myself."

Did what he did?

"I told Mama after it happened and she slapped me and said shut up. She called me fast, said she told me not to play outside when Uncle Marcel been drinking." Adrian grabs my arm. Her hand is still bandaged. "She never said that Ben. You have to believe me. She never told me not to play outside."

Play outside.

"I believe you," I say.

"Nobody believed me but my sister," she says.

"Sister," I repeat.

"She left a long time ago." Adrian bites her lip, nods. "She was my rock. My twin."

"You had a twin?" I say.

"Sorta. Yes. Not exactly. Not really. I just called her that."

I can't think of anything to say.

"Remember the day I called and asked if I could stay with you?" Adrian asks.

"We'd broken up, we hadn't spoken in ages, and I hadn't heard from you for months," I say. "Then Katrina. I thought you were dead. I spent a week watching CNN hoping to see your face in a crowd shot, at the Superdome, on a bus, anywhere, but I never did. I told my students that I'd have to answer the phone if anyone called during class. I couldn't sleep. I couldn't imagine a world without you in it. And then CNN moved on to other problems. Nobody called. I called in sick and got drunk for a week. Then I tried to move on."

"I never knew all of that," Adrian says.

"There's a memorial park for unclaimed victims," I say. "Somewhere around Canal Street. I always meant to go, but I couldn't do it. Then five years after the storm, you call. I thought I was dreaming." Colors rushed back into the gray world, the clanging that accompanied every voice vanished, the glass stuck in my chest fell to the floor. "I was just glad to hear your voice. To know you were okay." I say.

"I wasn't okay," Adrian says. "They locked me up. I watched my sister and Marcel and my mother all die. I lost it. My sister was all I had. She kept me steady. And then she was gone. So they threw me in a mental institution."

"She drowned in the flood?"

Adrian drains her champagne.

"She. She." Adrian shakes her head. "The day Marcel split me, I became two people. There was me getting," she points to the ground, "getting raped, and me," she points to the sky, "cold and alone."

Raped.

"She just stuck around, you know. Because it happened again. It happened a lot over the next few years. Nobody believed me but my sister," she says.

Years.

"So I just shut up."

"You didn't have a choice." Raped. "You were a kid."

"Uncle Marcel liked to be *first*," she hissed, glaring at him. "He got tired of me. I got too old. I thought he was my boyfriend and we would get married. Isn't that fucked up? I thought we would have babies."

My stomach churns. I rock forward and take a few breaths. Raped. My body feels feverish. The warm wind leaves me in a pool of my own sweat but takes nothing away.

"And the mental institution?" I ask.

"Yeah. I started screaming on the bus to Houston, so they took me off. I didn't even know where I was. And then I wound up in some hospital. My hand was bleeding, mama was dead, my sister was gone, I was a mess. They thought I cut myself, but I didn't. I would never do that."

"Your sister," I say. "Your sister you never saw until you were ten?"

"Yeah."

"You sister who didn't exist until you were ten."

"Why do you say it like that?"

"Like what?" I ask.

"Imaginary. Like she wasn't real."

"She wasn't real. I mean she was real to you, but she wasn't real real. You created her to deal with the stress."

"You don't believe me."

"Of course I believe you."

Adrian explodes. "What happened to me was real, alright Professor? Your stupid books don't have women like me but my life is real, I'm real."

"Whoa!" I say. "I'm trying to support you."

"She was real."

"You never had an actual sister. You made her up. You had good reasons for making her up, but she wasn't real."

"Fuck you."

"Adrian!"

"You have to be the dumbest Hotep of all time," she says.

"I've fucking had enough of people calling me Hotep today! What the fuck? I don't know what Hotep even means. First that crazy jogger, then Althea, now you."

Adrian stops, a brilliant brown hummingbird mid-flight, moving even when she's still. "Althea."

"Yeah."

"My mother's name."

"I remember. I met a woman named Althea today." The wind turns fierce. Leaves and small branches blow across the yard. A thick branch falls on Marcel's shoulder and breaks.

I have to raise my voice to be heard. "Maybe we should go in." The creaking noise starts again, just like before. Not like before. Louder, and deeper. Rain blows onto our faces and I know the answer before the taste hits my tongue. Saltwater.

"We have to get inside!" I yell.

"What?" Adrian says.

"Inside!"

Adrian looks up. Above us, aloft and afloat, impossible and always, real-real and not-real, the moving past, a collection of stories, the ash-black *Yemaya*. With a splintering sound, the ship tilts downward. Adrian screams. I pull her off the porch and dive for the ground. Defying every paradox, *Yemaya* flies like an arrow on the wind and hits our house with a deafening boom.

Butterpears

Between here and there, Adrian Dussett looked above the wrecked roof to see an ancient slave ship held aloft by the heads of the legendary tribe of Flying Africans who escaped bondage by leaping from disaster. These souls looked nothing like the glorious people she imagined while banished from New Orleans to her grandparents' porch in Okahika as a small girl so she could learn to believe in miracles. Their ashen skin spoke of long flights in cold air. Rags wrapped around privates or clutched by hand might have once been clothing. Some carried tattered sacks bulging with bananas, coconuts, and avocados. *Butterpears*, Adrian reminded herself. *They call them butterpears.*

Back then, as the story went, according to her granmé, who spun tales from the piano bench propped against the wrought iron pillar of her pink and white shotgun house, slavers attacked villages at night like silent ghosts who drank the blood of the living. The slavers whipped the proud Igbos or fierce Mandingoes or mystical Yoruba down long roads to the coast and loaded them onto their clipper, nicknamed *Yemaya* after the cries of so many in her belly. After a two-month voyage across the Atlantic, the slavers sold the entire tribe and their ship to a blubbery riverboat captain named Jenkins.

Red-faced and squat, clad in a white hat and planter's suit, astride his last horse, Jenkins fancied himself a direct descendant of Odysseus. Jenkins left the British Naval Orphanage at 8 and travelled the world as a cabin boy for the East India Company. The Mate let Jenkins cry until England sank under the slate waves. Then he seized young Jenkins by the neck. "Two kinds of men," the Mate growled. "You and me." Jenkins nodded quickly, and plotted his first unsuccessful revenge, followed by aborted mutinies, attempted murders, and failed coups until he grew old enough to defend himself.

Jenkins imagined his ascension from cabin boy to seaman to captain to planter, then Mayor, then Governor or Senator or some other befitting office. He dreamed of owning a plantation in America named Ithaca-on-the-Shore with white columns and a wishing well. His silver tongue might be able to leverage some wealthy woman. Southern cities teemed with unfortunate widows and willing young debutantes pliable to a hard-working man of industry like himself. Jenkins stole ashore and took up riverboat gambling, eventually winning the very boat he gambled on. He bet on horse races until he won a stable Hercules would envy. He frequented brothels of free women and slave women, where every deposit became an investment.

Yet true wealth lay in slaves. "Slaves are America's greatest asset, second only to the land itself," he declared after using a brothel girl. "Greater than railroads. Greater than banks. I must maneuver myself into position." Jenkins sold almost everything he owned: his whores, his riverboat, and every horse in his stable save the bay stallion he rode, all of his guns except the pistol, one last whip. "My ship has come in."

The ship transported enslaved humans across the Atlantic. Once, the ship had a Christian name, given to her by a long-dead captain when she transported cotton and rum. But using a thing changes a thing. Trip after trip, wave after wave, her human cargo begged for relief, any kind of help, from the one force they thought could help. *Ye-ma-ya*. After years at sea and uncounted songs and prayers to *Yemaya* from the captives, after docking in Brazil, Mexico, the Grenadines, Haiti, and every Southern port in America, after soaking up the blood and shit and semen of thousands, whatever name the ship once held vanished from all ledgers and manifests. Sailors and slaves called the ship *Yemaya*.

Jenkins wanted everything slaves granted: land, food, women, power. Although he already knew how one or two pretty slave girls could entertain a ship full of men, his plans passed beyond physical labor.

In the British Navy, Jenkins had seen dancing devils on African shores with his own eyes. Legends said the tribes could summon powerful forces at any time and command their power. According to the law and the coin he paid the slavers,

Jenkins owned the tribe now and all they produced. He owned their power. Jenkins wanted the tribe to show him black magic and demon worship.

Jenkins ordered the enslaved to produce the devil. They pretended not to understand. He shouted. He beat the men. He raped a small girl in front of her screaming parents. He slapped an old woman and shouted, "Devil! Give me devil!" Jenkins gripped the woman's neck and squeezed until her eyes bulged, determined to wring each tribesman to death if necessary.

"Boss," the old woman's grandson begged, "Bossman." The boy pleaded with Jenkins, cried, and even though the old woman sucked her teeth, the boy agreed to show the devil if Jenkins spared his grandmother. Jenkins unchained the boy and told him to get to work immediately. The shackles fell onto the wood planking and dissolved, leaving only a dark imprint where the hissing metal struck the deck. The boy gestured to Jenkins and indicated he would need fire, much fire, and women freed to dance, and a large draft animal, a mule or even an ox. Jenkins ignored the metallic tang in his mouth and said, "Tell my horse—"

Adrian's grandfather ambled onto the porch and let the door slam. "Don't go scaring the girl," he said.

"Pay him no mind honey. Grandpópa afraid of the truth."

As Moses Dussett stepped carefully in his best shoes across the sunken cinder blocks which led from the wooden porch to the family's mint green Lincoln Mark VI, he decided to pray extra hard for his precocious granddaughter who seemed to know the ends of lies before people started speaking.

"Hush up," Isadora Dussett muttered as her husband drove to Wednesday prayer meeting. "Girl needs to know how the world go." She looked at her granddaughter, overdeveloped for her age, too womanly and too young. Isadora had her first living child at 14 and hoed an entire field on her own the day before. This girl still played with dolls.

Life will toughen her up, the old woman reflected. Life will.

Jenkins unshackled three enslaved women and snatched up the girl. He put a pistol to the girl's temple. He raped her again. He would kill her without hesitation. The women wailed and pleaded, but they feared the stinking madman with the bulging eyes who couldn't smell melting iron. The enslaved made their preparations quickly. Jenkins thought of whipping the girl just for pleasure, but decided against it. Jenkins saw no need to over-exert himself. His gun kept everyone in line so he tossed his whip away. The leather soaked into the planking and left snaky, dark welts. The boy indicated he needed something from the hold. Jenkins sent a woman with him. They returned shortly, carrying a crate Jenkins didn't remember buying. The boy kicked it open and a startled dove flew out and landed next to Jenkins. An iron cauldron the size of a rich man's bathtub rolled out next, lolling around the deck until it came to a rest. The deck groaned miserably under the weight, but the cauldron held nothing.

Finally, Jenkins thought, getting somewhere.

He tightened his grip on the limp girl. The boy and the women dragged an iron plate from the crate and dropped it onto the deck. It made no sound. They built a fire on the plate and then attempted to place the cauldron on the fire. The heavy cauldron wouldn't move. Jenkins unlocked another enslaved man and ordered him to lift the cauldron. He failed. Jenkins saw his muscles straining and the veins on his black forehead bulge, but the cauldron stuck to the deck. The fire sputtered. Jenkins unlocked another enslaved, and another and another. Four enslaved men together could not lift the cauldron. Finally Jenkins dropped the girl and tried it himself. He lifted the cauldron alone and without effort. The copper basin felt impossibly light for something so large.

Jenkins remembered another story, about how King Arthur pulled a sword from a stone. Arthur married Guinevere and lived happily ever after in a castle with the Around Table and his friend Lancelot. Jenkins knew at that moment that the Lord Almighty meant him to lift the cauldron, marry a high-class girl with money, pass out pennies for children to throw into his wishing well at Ithaca-on-the-Shore, then go on to become Senator. He stood before the enslaved, proudly displaying his white strength. He opened his mouth to make a speech and noticed the escaped dove melting into a rubbery puddle near his boot heel. Some great invisible hand scorched the outlines of tiny feathers into the wood, intricate and beautiful, a dizzying array of whorls as each feather melted into the next and again and – it was a map.

A rugged coastline dotted with fragrant almond trees. Mountains filled with iron and gold. Diamonds glittering under secret river deltas. Paths leading to roads marked by subtle straight lines of coconut palms planted twelve steps apart for miles upon miles through the untamed jungle. Ruined gates of lost cities guarded only by screaming troops of chimpanzees. An ancient stone palace still echoing from the flute of an enchanted child; whispered conversations of courtiers frolicking on long red couches; the treasury stuffed with salt in great disks, sheaves of copper, and 144 bags of gold dust; the armory guarded by an army of conquered kings; a clay creature he could not name but seemed to exist only in words; a vast library preserved since ancient days, where the secrets of the Pharaohs and the Aztec hid in endless rooms of papyrus scrolls numbered in a counting system devised before the Greeks learned poetry; a temple built from quartz the color of strawberries in sweet cream; a university above the clouds reached on the backs of great spiders who demanded human blood for their passage; a harem filled with beauties from every corner of the world in every variety of hue and disposition who only awaited the call of their rightful lord; great tombs, farms and parklands, groves of ebony and camwood, all laced by long roads stretching across the world bringing trade and money and power to the hidden city.

Jenkins gasped and capered across the deck. The iron cauldron grew heavy, heavier, until Jenkins' joints popped and veins bulged from his legs and forehead. A demoness appeared inside the cauldron, bathing in human sweat. The tribe shrank away but Jenkins had no eyes for anything but his pigeon-map and the demoness. Jenkins lowered the cauldron and bowed like a courtier before his newfound Queen. He held her hand as the demoness stepped out of her bath, plump and naked, with a double chin, brown skin, long black locks, and heavy, erect breasts. Fluid dripped from her thighs. A flute sounded softly. She stood over the map and said, "I offer you pleasures not known since Adam."

Jenkins knelt. His jaw hung slack. His muscles felt impotent. Yet he retained the use of his tongue and spoke eloquently and long to the demoness: his plans, his vision, the map she stood on and the kingdom they would rule. Together. As man and wife. Long after the sun sank behind the soil, Jenkins spoke and plotted and promised while his beloved trembled in delight. Lesser men plied their brides with money and clothing. Jenkins kept human bodies in plenty and pledged them all.

She smiled. She caressed his shoulders, his chest, his fat belly. Jenkins kept speaking, but the words fell apart in his mouth and emerged as a long slurry of meaningless sounds. The demoness opened his pants and pulled out his erect penis. She lay down on the deck and drew Jenkins into her body.

Love, Jenkins thought, I have found love.

Jenkins floated aloft on the infinite waves of her hips, her thighs, her breasts, tossed to and fro, on top of her and in her and at her mercy all at once. He no longer cared about the tribe or their ridiculous map, and his plans for the Senate and Ithaca-on-the-Shore seemed like a child's fantasy. Only she mattered. He only wanted her. If all his years of humiliation and torment at sea, and all his years sniffing after better men's money ashore led to this moment, well Judas himself could not have struck a better bargain.

The demoness grew her legs long and wrapped them around the entire ship. She wrapped her arms around Jenkins, still talking, still talking, then shoved a finger down his throat.

Jenkins wailed.

She patted him on the back until he burped.

Jenkins struggled.

She curled around his wrists and ankles.

Her finger secreted seawater, at first a trickle Jenkins could swallow, then more, too much. She bucked wildly and the ship rolled over. The Africans screamed and held onto each other for dear life. She bucked again and a hurricane rolled across the shore. The ship crashed into the docks. Every shackle, iron, and chain fell from the captives belowdecks. Strange heat came from the metal. The hold caught aflame and the captives fled onto the listing deck. In the storm, they found their goddess.

Jenkins began to choke. Her finger forced his throat open. Help me, he seemed to say, or I love you. No one could say. She stroked his hair. I am drowning, Jenkins thought. I am dead. Her wild orgasm crushed his spine. She arose, clad in water, while Jenkins' corpse melted into the deck. Flames chewed through the holds. The air stank of melted iron. She looked at the people and whispered, "Go." Without pausing, the Flying Africans jumped from the deck and flew away, looking back to behold her crush the burning hull between her legs.

As the last of Jenkins melted, she sung an old sea chantey he'd heard once, long ago, as a child.

Say I, old man, ye horse shall die
Say I, old man, ye horse shall die
We'll drop him down to the depths of the sea
We'll drop him down to the bottom
We'll drop him down to the depths of the sea
We'll drop him down to the bottom
We'll sing him down with a long, cold roll
And we'll sing him down with a long, cold roll
And we'll sing him down with a long, cold roll
Til the sharks eat his body
And the devil take his soul.

PODCAST

Willie Cole's Stowage

Willie Cole is a well-known contemporary American sculptor and visual artist. Cole takes inspiration from Dadaist readymades and the reimagined objects found in Surrealist paintings of the 1920's. However, his work often moves in the realm of Postmodern appropriation and eclecticism, combining references to African and African-American imagery with American pop and consumer culture.

While living in an abandoned factory, Cole found the famous Brookes diagram that depicts 454 enslaved African shackled together in spaces just 10 inches high. Slave traders assumed a large percentage of the enslaved would not survive the passage, so they crammed as many as possible onto their ships to ensure a healthy profit. The Brookes diagram became a powerful weapon for the abolitionist cause in Britain and America.

Cole immediately envisioned the Brookes as an ironing board surrounded by icons of the tribes it carried. The tribes of the people of iron are the Sunbeams, the Silexes, and other brands, brands representing both a commercial enterprise and the marks made on enslaved people, ideas co-mingled in slavery and again in Cole's art. The iron marks also signify the transportation of enslaved African and the domestic labor performed by African American women. These scorches on plywood became his signature piece, *Stowage*. The iron itself is composed of three elements and represented by three African gods - Ogun, god of iron, Shango, god of fire, and Ye-ma-ya, the mermaid goddess, goddess of water.

BEN

Cold Hands,
Warm Heart

A heavy hotness presses me to the ground. My body parts lay around, disconnected and useless. Putting myself back together feels like one of those Yes/No flowcharts on the internet. Should I move? Yes. Does it hurt? Yes. Start over. Should I move? Yes. Does everything hurt? Yes. Can I wiggle my fingers? Yes. Both hands? Yes. Use the fingers to find the arms, the elbows, the shoulders. Push on the shoulders to see if they're still connected. Are my shoulders connected? Yes. Touch the ribs. Is this a good idea? No, it hurts like fuck. Say ow.

"Sonofabitch!"

Pain curls my body up into a ball. Now my knee hurts. My bones grind on each other when I move. Something stinks. I hope that's not me. The ground heaves up and down like waves at sea and I'm soaked to the skin, by sweat or seawater or burst pipes, I'm not sure. I inhale deeply, and the pain in my ribs expands until it envelops my whole body and for a moment, just a moment, displaces my position as master and commander of myself. For a moment, the pain takes charge, calls the shots, gives the orders, and I, me, the person I think I am, gets shoved out and set aside. I look at myself, broken and bloody in the debris of my home, controlled by pain. Ben, I say, you'll never be handsome or a good dancer. So you need to be smart and get a good job. That's the only way you'll attract a woman. Adrian stays with you because she needs a safe place to live, not because she loves you. You'll never find the one little thing everyone else figured out. You're no one's special someone. But whatever happens, you won't figure anything out laying on the ground. Get up, I say. Ben, get up.

I roll onto my knees and vomit into another puddle of vomit. So it was me. My ears ring. I try to crawl away, but the weight of the world rests on my back. I move a few steps and the ground heaves again. Breathe, I think. In and out. My ribs send sharp spikes through my lungs and back, and my knee apparently catches on fire.

My phone begins playing the last podcast I listened to, the one about Willie Cole. "...the reimagined objects found in Surrealist paintings..." I want to turn it off. I will turn it off. In a minute. First things first. I take a few shallow breaths and push myself onto my feet.

The lawn is a mess. Roof shingles and insulation lay scattered on the grass. Fallen tree limbs lay everywhere. The car looks fine, but we can't leave without chainsaws to cut the downed trees. Marcel stands right where we left him, and the little peach tree I planted is still standing.

The crisp taste of a peach floods my mouth, sweet, tangy. I really want a peach.

Like a slow-motion replay, I remember *Yemaya* hurtling towards us, too fast to stop, too impossible to stop, me running, diving for the ground, pulling Adrian out of the way. Adrian. I pulled her with me. She should be here. She should be right here.

"Adrian!"

I start throwing pieces of debris to the side.

"Adrian!" Holy crap, she can't be dead, no, no, this is my fault. "Marcel, help me!" I yell. He doesn't move.

"Adrian!" I scream again and again as I dig through the debris, not caring if I get hurt, not caring if pain casts my soul out for all eternity as long as Adrian lives. I can't go through this again.

"Ben!" Adrian answers. "Ben, where are you?" Small raindrops fall on my face.

I let out a huge sigh of relief. "Over here," I say.

"Are you alright?" she asks.

"Not really," I answer. "You?"

"We're fine," she answers.

I turn towards her, but pain shoots through my legs. She's alright, that's the important thing. Small branches and leaves rain down over my back. I feel like I'm being watched. I am being watched. Something sees me from above, but not the cicadas. They've gone silent. And the Cheeper-Cheeper Tape bird always announces itself. I know what's looking. I don't want to know what's looking. I don't need to look up because I know what's there, though some part of me hopes it's not there and if I just turn my head up I'll see nothing. If I take a good long look, this whole mess will happen somewhere else to people I don't know. Or I'll look up and see the night sky, look at my house and the unfilled trees and see Adrian, and we'll go inside our perfectly intact home and watch Netflix while I tell her about my day of laundry and grading and cat finding, and she talks about work and clients, and we drink a bottle of wine before bed.

I can't help myself. I look up. *Yemaya* looms over my head, rimmed in soft light. She's long, perhaps half the length of a football field, but her hull is cracked and scarred. Her nose is buried in the wreck of my house, and her end sticks out over the street. I'm about midway between the ends, but I can't tell for sure. She's held aloft by what's left of our house and a few small trees. If she falls, she'll kill me. Still, I can't help but admire her symmetry, her elegance. She must have been a thing of beauty once.

Now I do see the house. Some of the walls have collapsed. The porch swing snapped in half, and every window blew out. The front door hangs from one hinge, and a light rain soaks everything else. Our home is gone. Our home is gone. Where will we go? Everything we own is gone. We have our bank accounts, one credit card, our car, and a cat. Was Free Cookie inside when the house collapsed? I don't know.

Just then, it occurs to me that ships are always female. That's what I need, another complicated woman in my life.

Maybe they don't come any other way.

"Adrian," I said, "I love you. I'm sorry."

"Sorry for what?"

"For everything," I say. For bringing this on us, for not knowing how to prevent it, for getting you caught up in my problems, for sitting on the couch sulking day after day while you work, for being a lousy dancer. "For everything." Those are probably my last words. Not exactly original, but from the heart. If I'd thought to write a will, it would declare my death as one small mystery among larger questions and spell out my tombstone: Here Lies Ben Hughes, Killed by *Yemaya*.

Adrian climbs over the wreckage into view, somehow changed into workout clothes: white sneakers, blue yoga pants, red sports top with stars. Adrian takes my face in her hands. "Don't worry about it, Hotep." she says. "I'm fine."

"Your hands are freezing," I say.

"Cold hands, warm heart," she says.

Her voice is off. I can't explain it. A flying slave ship demolishing your house would make anyone's voice sound strange, sure, but she's not frightened, or tired, or shell-shocked. She's perfectly calm, steady, like a surfer on a huge wave.

"Easy Hotep," she says. "Take a moment."

I look at Adrian. It's as if her face lived a different life. The bones, the muscles, the eyes and lips are all the same, but the motivations behind the bones, the reasons why she smiles or frowns or sucks her teeth have changed. Adrian wears a mask of herself. I look from side to side, trying to see the edges. And she's cold, ice cold.

"Almost there, Hotep."

My phone repeats, "The iron itself is composed of three elements."

She's Adrian, but she's not Adrian. I've seen her before. "Wait," I say. "You're that jogger from yesterday."

"What gave it away," she asks. "My kicks?"

"Where's Adrian?"

"I'm right here," she says and grabs my arm. Coolness. Coldness. Ice. The heavy hotness fades as if I'd just walked into a freezer. I shiver and clench my teeth to keep from chattering.

"I don't know who you are," I start.

"She just told you, Hotep. I'm her twin."

Yemaya shifts a fraction of an inch to the left.

"That's impossible," I say. Her twin was never real. Her twin is dead. And this woman is not quite Adrian's twin. She's a close resemblance, sure, but not exact. Something in Adrian's face draws me in, makes me feel closer, and something in not-Adrian's face puts me on guard. "Where's Adrian? Where's my Adrian?"

"You didn't recognize me before," she says. "I thought you was fucking with me. You looked me in the face and didn't know me."

"Where's Adrian?"

"You don't own her, Hotep."

"Ben!" a man yells.

"What have you done with Adrian?" I yell.

"Pulled her out of your mess," she shouts.

"My mess?" I shout back. "I didn't ask for any of this."

The man yells again. "Ben!"

Yemaya shifts a fraction of an inch to the right.

"A powerful weapon," my phone says.

"You knew and you never told her," the jogger says. "How hard was it to say, 'Hey baby, I saw a flying motherfucking ship'? Huh? How hard was it to say 'I saw your dead mama wandering around town?'"

I don't have any answer.

Yemaya shifts another fraction of an inch to the left.

"Ben!" he yells again. I know that voice, I know I know that voice, but before I can speak, Adrian, my Adrian, shoves the jogger aside. I reach around hold her to me, her chest to my chest, my face deep in her hair, our hips locked together. Falling leaves swirl around us in a silent, green halo. She's muddy and her dress is torn. We hold each other, trembling like flowers in a David Bowie song. This, this, this. This is all.

"Ben!" The man yells again. "Ben!"

"Jackson?" I shout back. "Is that you?"

"Hey, Jackson," Adrian says.

Yemaya rests on a half-broken branch.

"Look out, y'all," Jackson yells. "Look out y'all!" Jackson runs towards me. The jogger stands and gets in Adrian's face. "You shove me out for Hotep? No job, no life, can't do shit."

"Back the hell up," Adrian says, turning toward her. I've never seen her so angry. "You've been gone for years. Do not accuse me."

"Dammit, y'all," Jackson shouts, but too late.

Yemaya floats down from above, graceful as a Monarch butterfly on an angel's nose, and lands squarely on our heads. Adrian, Jackson, the jogger, and I try to look at each other, but we're stuck. This is another one of those moments home training doesn't prepare you for. What would my mother say if she saw us now, soaked to the skin, covered in mud, with a slave ship balanced on our heads? She'd tell me to quit smoking dope. Or give me some dope. I imagine her in her Easter Sunday best, pulling a joint out of her hat, then putting it back, then pulling it out again. I giggle.

"The hell's so funny, Hotep?" the jogger asks.

I start laughing and can't stop. "Should we take drugs, or should we stop taking drugs?" Adrian looks at me and laughs. Jackson laughs, and even the jogger smiles and laughs a bit, which makes Adrian laugh more, and then I'm laughing at her and Jackson's laughing at me and we're all helpless.

"I could smoke a bowl to-day!" Jackson says. Now we're all laughing, really laughing, as *Yemaya* rests lightly on us. Adrian laughs so hard she doubles over, or she would, except her hair catches on the hull of the ship. Instead of doubling over, Adrian doubles up, like someone doing knee raises at the gym.

"Ow!" she says. "My hair is caught."

"Let me help you," the jogger says. She takes a step towards Adrian, but the rough hull digs into her hair until she can only move a step in any direction. Now they're both stuck.

"You're stuck?" Adrian says. "I thought you couldn't get stuck like me."

The jogger, for once, says nothing.

"Adrian," I say, "You're gonna have to explain the twin thing to me again."

"You got a twin sister?" Jackson exclaims.

"It's a long story," Adrian and the jogger reply.

"What your name?" Jackson asks. Before she can reply, Jackson takes a step and yells, "Ow! Goddamn!"

"What the -" I ask.

"I'm stuck!"

"You're bald! How can you get stuck?"

"Nigga, I don't know!"

"I don't like that word," the jogger says. "It's disrespectful."

"My head stuck on the bottom of a slave ship is disrespectful," Adrian says.

"Hang on," I say and take a step, but the hull jerks my entire body back.

We're all stuck under the ship in a rough line. I'm last, looking at the back of everyone's head. Next is the jogger, then Adrian, then Jackson. I have an idea. I reach up and find a patch of hair, then twiddle my fingers until I'm down to one.

"Okay. I'm gonna pull one hair off the ship. Here goes. One, two—" I say, breathing hard, and then yank. Stinging pain whips across my head and neck, reaching down my back. I feel like I've been lit on fire. Every sound bounces around the inside of my skull, gathers strength, and flies out of my mouth as a wordless howl. It's a few seconds before I can make sense of what anyone says to me.

"Ben?"

"Can you hear us?"

"Ben, are you bleeding?" Adrian asks.

I groan. "You're right, I need a haircut," I say.

"We can't just stand here," the jogger says.

"We need some scissors," Jackson says.

"What are you even doing here Jackson," I ask. "I thought you were traveling with the team."

"Crazy weather tonight, so the team plane got grounded. I came by to see if you had that photo but—" Ethiopia looks up at *Yemaya*. "I'll get back at Moms later. The magazine will go crazy for this."

"Hold up," I say, more forcefully than I meant. "If anyone is writing about how *Yemaya* landed on my head, it's me."

Yemaya presses down. I have to push up to stay still.

"*Ye-ma-ya*? You've already named the ship?" he says.

"Yeah," I say.

Adrian says, "On your head? It landed on all of us." She adjusts under the weight.

"You need a better name than that."

"That's her name," I insist.

"I got a name," Jackson says. "Booty Pirate."

"She's not a pirate ship."

"How do you know she's a she?"

"All ships are shes," I say.

"That's some reductionist bullshit," Jackson says, as if 'reductionist' was a word he used in everyday conversation. "You're subscribing to gender binary thinking."

Yemaya shifts herself around. A little to the left, a little to the right. Each of us shifts our bodies to compensate.

"Yeah, Hotep," the jogger says.

"Wait a minute," I say, "since when is this about me?"

"Ben Hotep, your stories are always about you," Adrian says.

"Ben Hotep!" Jackson exclaims. "Wait, did we know you during the Battle? Back in the day?"

"First of all, I do not subscribe to gender binary thinking, alright?" I say. "Ships are shes. Female. I didn't make the rule."

"Gender is a social performance," Jackson says.

"Gender is—since when did you become a gender expert?"

"I know shit, my nigga."

"He knows his shit, Hotep," the jogger says.

"The fuck is a Hotep?" I yell.

Yemaya rolls starboard. We're all dragged off our feet as the ship demolishes one of the stately magnolias next door. I trip, but the ship holds me aloft. For the first time, I can hear past the four of us again. Voices shout. Cicadas chirp loudly. Sorry guys. You worked for years to maintain your clock and now it's all gone.

"A Hotep," Jackson says, "is one of those Afrocentric brothers always saying like 'my beautiful African queen' and 'we were kings and queens in Africa' and all that bullshit."

"You say that!"

"A Hotep," Jackson says, "believes in black liberation as long as black men get liberated and black women make dinner."

"I cook all the time."

Yemaya rolls into the Strickland Mansion and wrecks something I can't see.

"Right now? Really?" Adrian asks. "Unless y'all want to answer a bunch of questions about why there's a ship on our heads and why we destroyed half of Historic Downtown Northport, we got to go."

Half of downtown? Under the hull, we can turn our heads somewhat, about half the range we'd have without a ship sitting on us. *Yemaya* did far more damage than I realized. The Strickland Mansion is wrecked, and the office across the street is a pile of bricks now. Broken trees and power lines lay everywhere. Her keel dug deep ruts in the street. I doubt a regular car could get past now.

"Can we move?" Jackson asks?

"Let's try," Adrian replies.

"Which way?" I ask.

"That way," Adrian says, waving her hand towards the river. "Marcel!" she shouts. Marcel wades through the wreckage towards us. "Walk," Adrian says. "In front of us. Where I can see you."

We wade across the yard, pushing our legs like people in deep surf. We have to concentrate, clench fists, and push, like pushing a very heavy car with our heads. After just a few steps, my heart pounds wildly and my knees shake. I'm soaked to the skin. I should go to the gym more often. Adrian, in the front of our line, gives directions by waving a hand right or left. No one talks now. The jogger follows her, then me, then Jackson. We navigate the ship into the street and pause. Everyone is out of breath.

"Where are we going?" the jogger asks.

"That way," Adrian says.

"Let's get into The Through," I suggest. "It's the only place big enough to hide." And maybe we'll find some help. If nothing else, we should find Althea's bench and cooler. It suddenly occurs to me that the last time I saw Althea, she hauled *Yemaya* by rope, alone. She's not here now. Something may have happened to her. I don't see the rope now. It also occurs to me that the last time I saw Althea, she was dead.

"The Through," Jackson says. "You mean what's left of Okahika, Alabama."

"Sure," I reply. "That's what Randolph called that end of town." Adrian waves her hand and we all push *Yemaya* forward, step by step, down towards the end of town. The weight is incredible. I feel like I'm about to have a heart attack. Sirens wail. Our feet sink into the asphalt, leaving deep footprints. A slight breeze passes under the ship, raising a putrid stench. I want to gag, but I'm afraid of pulling my hair out again.

"Randolph, yeah." Jackson says. "Did y'all get out to Granny Mary's place?"

"Should have told us phones don't work out there," Adrian says.

As we talk, *Yemaya* lifts herself.

"They don't? Shit, I didn't know. Truth is," Jackson says, "she scares me. I ain't been out there since I was a kid."

"She scared us too," I say.

"I wasn't scared," the jogger says.

"You weren't there," I snap back, but then I wonder, am I sure? Adrian's twin either never existed or she died. Or she exists and she's alive. Or she existed, died, and came back. Or she existed and never existed and lived and died. Has she been the one flirting with Ethiopia and laughing at his jokes all this time? Was she the one fighting with me tonight? If I never saw both of them at the same time, would I know Adrian was Adrian and the jogger was the jogger? Why didn't I recognize the jogger before?

"We drank some scotch and she gave us plants," the jogger said. Does she know everything Adrian knows, feel everything Adrian feels, or has she been spying on us? I wish Adrian would say something. I can't blame her though. My lungs may crack open under the strain. I can't imagine how she's doing.

Yemaya loses lightness and presses down again.

"How did she look?" Jackson asks.

"Fine," the jogger says. "I mean, we never saw her before, but she looked just fine."

"Liar," Adrian says. "You're a damn liar."

"You got a great ass, Jackson," the jogger says.

"Squats," Jackson replies.

Yemaya lifts herself again.

"Wait," I say. "Wait."

Everyone stops moving.

"No, keep going," I say. "But talk while we go." Everyone starts walking again. *Yemaya* presses down on us, grinding our spines.

"Talk about what?" the jogger asks.

"The people of iron are the Sunbeams," my phone says.

"Anything, doesn't matter," I say.

"Is the ship getting lighter?" Adrian asks.

"It's us," I say. "Our voices. When we talk, the ship lifts. Goes higher. We just need to keep talking."

Jackson slips in a shallow puddle. "Ow!" he says. We all stop moving. Something falls from his shirt - a tattered black leather medallion, in the shape of the continent of Africa. Those were all the rage back in college.

"You still have one of those?" Adrian asks.

"This?" Jackson says. "This ain't just some Africa medallion. This is the original Africa medallion. It's how Ben and I met."

"Are you serious? Ben has a story he hasn't told me?" Adrian asks.

"You never told her about the Battle?" Jackson asks.

I just wave at him vaguely. "You're my best friend," I say, "Stuck with me and my girlfriend and her doppelgänger under a flying slave ship after we've sacked our own town. You tell her about the Battle."

I look up at him. He stands straight up, and his wet shirt reveals his back muscles. He looks good. He always looks good. He really could play Indiana Jones if he tried. But he's a talker, and extroverted in a way I'll never really understand. And we need a talker to keep *Yemaya* aloft. If I have a story worth telling, it's deep inside me, leaking out drop by drop. Eventually the drops will form a trickle and I'll follow, past the edge of town, down to the river, where I'll jump in and see what happens. If I could stand still, I'd feel subtle changes in gravity, my perception of myself and my place in this world, moving in a current that doesn't care if I go this way or that way as long as I go.

Okay, I think. Okay. Okay.

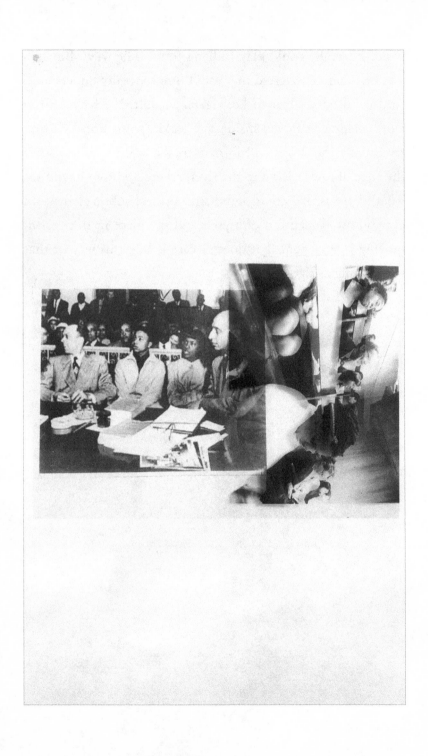

BEN

The Africa Medallion War, or How Hughes became Hotep

We trudge along in our odd way—me astern, the jogger and Jackson amidships, Adrian forward. Jackson says we met in college, but I felt like I already knew him then. When did we meet? Childhood, college, grad school, work? Ethiopia Jackson has always been with me and annoying as he is sometimes, I hope he always will be. He's the other side of my coin.

"So," he begins, "1990. Everyone was rocking the De La Soul look. Afrocentric. Bright colors, short dreads, Africa medallions. I'm in college, right? University of Texas at Austin, full scholarship but that didn't mean shit back then because tuition was only like $1000 a semester. You could make bank delivering pizza. Everyone had a hustle. So I'm on the Drag, this section of Guadalupe Street that runs in front of the campus. There was supposed to be a big anti-apartheid rally on the West Mall—our designated protest area. That part of campus held the biggest Vietnam protest of the Sixties on any college campus, just thousands and thousands of people flooding onto the West Mall. Back then, the West Mall was just a wide sidewalk set on a long slope with buildings on both sides and a set of steps at the top of the hill. The steps lead to the building with the President's office, or they did. After Vietnam, they walled off the West Mall and put trees all over in giant planters. Then they blocked off those stairs, so they literally lead nowhere. See that? Fucking stairs to nowhere.

"Skip back ahead. Walls, trees, stairs to nowhere. We roll with it. We didn't even know the campus got changed until later. So I'm walking down to the protest. UT Divest! We wanted the University to stop investing in companies that supported apartheid. Or against the white frats raping women and beating up Latinos. Or against some racist Law School professor. Austin had this hippie liberal reputation, but that town had issues, know what I'm saying?

"I hustled tuition by selling all that Afrocentric stuff: incense, candles, dashikis, little booklets, medallions, cowrie shell jewelry, posters, pretty much anything. You gotta remember, before 1990, most people thought the Cosby Show was about as Afrocentric as it got. I had tapes too: Zulu Nation, Native Tongues, X-Clan, A Tribe Called Quest, all that, on a little table out across the Drag in this little open plaza next to a bakery, right across from the entrance to the West Mall. So naturally, everyone met at my table before going to the protests.

"I had these huge Afrocentric sheets, right? Like big wall hangings. 'The Kemetic Womb of Eternal Life', that was my favorite. An ankh on one side and a woman's internals on the other side. The round part was the uterus, the straight part was the vagina or portal of life or whatever, and the little crossbars were fallopian tubes. But the one everyone remembered was these two Africans, a man and a woman, with like Pharaoh headdresses and loincloths. She had big tits and a loincloth bikini. And they were holding up a giant ankh. The title of that one was 'Hotep'. Ben here used to stand next to it and try to mack on all the girls buying incense, so we all started calling him Ben Hotep."

Adrian and the jogger laugh. *Yemaya* flew along lightly in the breeze. I'd completely forgotten about this whole incident, blocked it from my mind really, and now the whole era floods my memory.

"You were Ben Hotep back in the day?" the jogger asks. "I was right the whole time."

"He wanted to be," Jackson says. "See, I dressed good— round, colored John Lennon glasses, short dreads, soul patch, and my Africa medallion. Black leather, hand sewn, leather string. The medallion, that was the A-Bomb-diggity, you hear me? I had one, so Ben had to have one. He was still rocking his Cosby sweater."

Adrian and the jogger laugh again. "Cosby sweater!"

"We are not talking about this," I say.

My podcast springs to life again. "…combining references to African and African-American imagery with American pop and consumer culture." I mash my fingers into the phone until it stops.

"Anyway, I didn't have any," Jackson says. "I'm like, 'Sold out my brother, but can I interest you in some bean soda?'

"Ben's like, 'You misspelled fallopian. I need a medallion.' I'm like, 'My African Brother in Power, come back tomorrow.' You know how many Africans bought my bullshit? None. You know how much power we had? None. Almost none. When you 20, you got your feet and your voice so we protested. That's the power we had.

"I heard about another protest scheduled for the next day. I figured I'd get some more medallions, set up early, and get that protest fly. Fl-y. F-L-Why. I did not figure on me and Ben starting the Africa Medallion War."

Jackson turns his head and body under the ship until he faces all of us, lit by flashing red and blue lights. He walks backwards. "Looks like a tornado hit down there. Bunch of people walking around. Police, paramedics."

We all turn ourselves so we face back the way we came. The sensation feels like being twirled on a string. Looking back, we can see the damage. Several buildings have collapsed, and fallen trees lay everywhere.

"Should we go back?" Adrian asks.

"Until we get this ship off our heads, we're not much help," I say. Without saying anything else, the jogger, Adrian, and I turn ourselves so we're facing Jackson and The Through. We cast shadows across his body. In the alternating red and blue light, his face appears, disappears, reappears.

"Let's keep moving," Jackson says, breaking the spell.

"The Africa Medallion War started on September 14, 1990. I was dating this hot girl I'd met the night before. She'd been at a post-protest party wearing Coca-Cola striped pants and a t-shirt that said 'FCK all I need is U'. We had sex all night and into the next morning, and then I got some sleep. I woke up and she was still there so we became a thing. Poetry major. She was reading a book about Leopold Senghor and the Negritude movement. I'd never heard of Negritude, so Poetry explained that Negritude was like the original Afrocentrism, like a bunch of Africans were like 'why judge ourselves by European standards, let's judge ourselves by African standards' and they did it. They got like, 'this is what beauty looks like where we come from, this is music, this is dancing.' She read me something that changed me, for real. Senghor described a statue as columns of black honey. Ain't even poetry, just a cat describing a statue. 'Two themes of sweetness sing an alternating song. / The breasts are ripe fruits. / The chin and the knees, the rump and the calves are also fruits or breasts. / The neck, the arms and the thighs are columns of black honey.' Columns of black honey.

"I'm like, 'That's what you look like. She like, 'Bullshit.' Then we had sex some more until she fell asleep. I got up, grabbed a quick shower, took the book, and headed back to my spot. I figured I'd show the people some original blackness, and then put Columns of Black Honey on a sheet with the loincloth girl and make some money. I called Ben like, 'my man, take the table and hold my spot until I get ready.'

"Ben like, 'Dog.'

I get there and he got a LINE, goddammit, a line down the motherfucking block. I ain't even set up yet. Everybody wanted Africa medallions. Shit's made in China, nobody cares. Ben stood right behind the table.

"I was like, 'What up, my man?'

"He pointed to the line like, 'To the East my brother, to the east.' I was like, 'Chill Hotep. Help me set up and I'll give you a medallion for free.' Ben like, 'Aight.'

"We broke out the table, the candles, the incense, the sheets, all that. I ordered the medallions from a catalogue but they didn't have any pictures, just descriptions. 'Africa shape ornament, 3.5", leather, like that. I opened the box and saw they sent *two* kinds: regular black ones, and some Pan-Africa medallions in red, gold and green. And I looked the line and saw all the protest leaders waiting to get medallions, and I was like let me make me some money. We set up, and Ben picked a black medallion, cause he's already wearing a black shirt. I sold everything I got. I went to the West Mall. All the speakers got Africa medallions. Some got black, some got tricolor.

Who gives a damn, right? One Love. But the speeches—the speeches were different. I mean, they talked about apartheid and Nelson Mandela and the Angola 3 and all that, but you could tell that they were really only talking to the in-crowd. All of us ins with medallions kinda shifted to the left side of the podium, and everyone without a medallion stood on the right. Then another speaker came to talk about the MOVE organization in Philly. I got no people in Philly, so I looked for something to take my edge off. I saw this girl, nice booty, and she wasn't paying attention neither. She started checking me out and I was like 'damn.' So I pushed my way over to her and asked if she wanted to get the revolution going."

"You tried to hook up? At a rally?" the jogger asks.

"A woke mind need a woke body," Jackson says. "She's with it. I was like, 'My beautiful Nubian Queen, let us explore the mysteries of the Kemetic Womb of Eternal Life,' when she saw my black medallion, she got this look—" Jackson turns to us and sneers, eyebrows raised, lips curled. "—and pushed off. See, she's got a *tricolor* medallion."

"I was like, I sold you that medallion. You bought your expression of blackness from me! But it was too late. We were on different sides, and I didn't even know.

"Ain't shit else to do, so I listened to the speech. I don't remember the cause, I just remember the jokes. Speakers divided us into the conscious people and the Cosbys. To be conscious, you had to carry Mother Africa over your heart. Aight, that's good for sales. The Cosbys just took whatever the white man gave them. The Cosby sweaters got pissed off and left. And speaking of the white man, the cops started acting up so we moved to the after-party.

"The real shit went down at the after-party. We drank, smoked weed, and planned the next action. Normally, they let in anyone who was down, even the Cosbys. But this party is different, because they only let in people with medallions. And inside, the black medallions were on one side of the party and the tricolor medallions were on the other side. Blacks shaking hands with blacks, drinking 40s, making jokes with blacks, giving side eye to the tricolors. Tricolors smoking weed, throwing those big Rasta hugs, talking love and peace and nonviolence, but only with other tricolors. And that girl from the rally? She was over on the other side, letting some other brother with a tricolor medallion explore the mysteries. I was like, let me the hell out of here so I slipped out and go back to Poetry's place.

"She opened the door and guess what? She was wearing a tricolor medallion too, except hers got a picture of Bob Marley. I didn't even know I had medallions with photos. Poetry looked at my black medallion, says, 'whatever' and shuts the door in my face."

We're over halfway to the hole in the fence. I don't remember being as interesting as Jackson says, in college or any other time in my life. Jackson's voice lifts *Yemaya* as we walk. The ship rotates slowly in the light wind. If this keeps up, I'll wind up in front and Jackson will bring up the rear. Our toes barely touch the ground. We can turn and chat with each other as long as the story keeps going.

Adrian's yellow dress flutters in the breeze. Under her, small flowers burst through the asphalt and bloom in the middle of the night. Cicadas fall from her feet and get back to work, rebuilding the clock of the world. Her long legs stretch out and for the first time since this all started, her face relaxes into a wide smile—our goddess at the prow.

I can't see Marcel, but I hear his slow shuffle in front of us. The jogger stands straight up. What was that Old Testament saying? A pillar of smoke by day, a pillar of fire by night. The jogger is our pillar of water and ice. We don't have a name for her. I start to ask Adrian what her name is, but Adrian looks so peaceful that I can't disturb her. If Adrian never named her, maybe she doesn't need a name.

Jackson blows the wind into our sails. The police lights slow down, lighting Jackson's face one at a time: red, blue, rage, sorrow, hot, cold. When people carved masks, I think, his face right now is what they sought. He frowns.

Angry voices echo down the street. I can't make out what the voices want, but I know who they are. Pats and the Strickland brothers rant in one voice. Now I can hear them better. They never had this kind of problem before. The blacks tore off the roof and wrecked the trees.

Yes, I think. I put on my Giant Black Man suit and busted through the roof. Then I stole some shit and slept with all their wives at once.

Oh right, no. I'm right here.

Jackson says, "Come on, before these fools decide to follow us."

Adrian says, "Will we be safer in the Through?"

Jackson says, "I'm not sure. But it's better than here."

"I was never into the Afrocentric thing," Jackson says, "until I went to jail for my hustle before the hustle—practicing law without a license. I advertised myself as a divorce lawyer, then got all up in some divorcée booty and they paid *me* for the D. Until some angry, soon-to-be-ex-husband followed his wife to the Law Offices of Ethiopia Jackson, Esq., conveniently located off campus at the Motel 6. He took pictures. He showed them to the judge. The judge ordered an investigation. The State of Texas had no records of an Ethiopia Jackson taking the bar exam.

"I'm like, 'That's how I file a motion.' Denied. I'm like, 'My client never objected.' Denied.

"I'm like, 'This whole court is out of order.' Denied. I pled no contest and got ten days in jail, with time off for service to the legal community.

"In processing, I sat next to a man with a black Africa medallion tight around his neck. When the guards ordered us to strip, the man took off everything but the medallion. The guard ripped it off the man's neck. The man whupped that guard until blood flew across the room. Other officers ran in and beat the man down with batons. They carried the man away and I never saw him again. After the fight, I took my Flavor-Flav clock off and slipped the medallion under my suit. I thought a man who would fight cops for a medallion would pay anything to get it back, but you know what? Died in custody. He wasn't that hurt. I mean he was hurt but not dead the last time I saw him. They hauled him out kicking and screaming. Motherfucking cops. Ben picked me up when I got out, and I dropped the lawyer act and start selling Afrocentrism.

"So the day after we start selling tricolor medallions, I found Ben Hotep holding down my spot on the sidewalk. I needed to get set up. Rallies always drew customers, and from what I heard at the party, another one was coming. I needed a new medallion; something that will get me places with Poetry. Ben's always thinking ahead and he'd already ordered the newest freshest. The truck delivered it right to the sidewalk: a bigger tricolor medallion, with tricolor stitching and a photo of Marcus Garvey. Ben took care of the table, and I put Garvey on and went back to Poetry's place.

"I'm the shit, right? Mar-cus Gar-vey. She wasn't there, so I went to the rally and what did I see? Some motherfucker wearing the biggest Toussaint L'Overture medallion I ever saw. Must have been a foot long, with gold stitching, and - I ain't shitting you - it glowed. Like there was beams of light coming from Toussain't L'Overture. I saw it. And then next up—I can't believe it—it's Poetry.

She like 'My name is Mfungu. Black Studies on every syllabus!' She had on a new medallion too, a giant size Kwame

Nkrumah that she hung over her belly. Poetry held up Kwame Nkrumah, glued a picture of Cleopatra onto his face, and she like, 'Where are our mothers? Where is Madame C.J. Walker? Where is Harriet Tubman? Where is Queen Nefertiti? Where is Sojourner Truth? Where is Rosa Parks?'

"Oh snap! Poetry was protesting me. She saw me in the crowd, pointed, and said 'Now here come dis bitch.'

"Oh hell no. I headed back to my table, and found a dozen cats all selling different medallions. I was like, 'Shit Ben, now everybody's in on this.'

"Ben was like, 'Keep it cool. They working for us.' And I was about to say what's this us Negro, but turns out, Ben Hotep's a criminal mastermind. Ben ordered everything they had in that catalogue. That truck I saw, with the box of medallions, that was just the first of many deliveries. Ben Hotep hired a bunch of folks in line, men and women, and set them up with tables. If you didn't see it happen, you'd think they were the competition. Women selling black soap and natural hair care shouting about cultural appropriation at the women selling extensions and nail polish yelling about standards of beauty and fake it 'til you make it. Men selling fake Egyptian scrolls yelling about authenticity. The black frats each had a table with their letters on robes, hats, bumper stickers, yelling at each other about consumerism. Get this shit—Ben planned those arguments. He wrote the motherfuckers, made copies, sold them for a few bucks each. The more black people argued, the more we sold: Nefertiti, Cleopatra, loincloth bikini girls, sandalwood, ankhs, medallions, everything.

"Ben kept going, so I went back across the street to the rally and that shit was ugly. Someone threw a bottle at Poetry. An event organizer rushed onto the platform to shield her. Ben had just delivered his special commission: a four-foot long white leather medallion featuring a hand-painted portrait of Haille Selassie, trimmed in gold thread, with white leather thongs for the neck, wrists, and ankles. Selassie meant to unveil his masterpiece at the end of the rally but the crowd got too wild. He waddled onto the stage. The medallion hung around his neck but he had left one leg lace undone. The fool tripped and fell on his face. His crew jumped up and accused someone of tripping him. That's when the fight broke out.

"The Selassies held the stage first. The Marleys owed their allegiance the patron saint of Rastafarianism, so they pushed forward. The Garveyites aligned with the Malcolm X contingent and outflanked the Marley-Selassie coalition. A few MLKs played peacemaker, failed, and then declared the MLK medallions as the only true medallions. They stripped medallions from everyone else, starting with L'Overtures. An MLK put his hands on a Cleopatra. She took off her shoe and beat that man down. The Garvey-X faction went after the MLKs, saying they were protecting Cleopatra.

Miss Cleo was like, 'Attica!' and kicked some MLKs in the nuts until they started crying. The Selassies allowed the Marleys to protect their turf, but refused to let any Marleys get onstage. The Marleys jumped the stage and started fighting the Selassies.

"In the rush, I found Poetry aka Mfungu aka Cleopatra. I was like, 'Baby, let's get out of here.' The sun came down behind her. Sweat ran down Poetry's legs and I got it, I really got what Senghor meant by columns of black honey. Then a Cosby sweater jumped out of the bushes and clocked me in the jaw. I went down. He stood over me all like, 'Too Black, Too Strong.' I passed out.

"I woke up under a tree after the Africa Medallion War ended. 26 minor injuries, 8 concussions, 3 arrests, and 450 hours of collective community service. Apartheid lasted until '94. All the Africa medallions lay crushed on the pavement, except this one." Jackson pulls out his tattered black Africa medallion. "The original."

We reach the entrance floating, laughing at his ridiculous story, lifted off our feet by *Yemaya* as she completes her slow turn in the air. The entrance looks exactly like it did the day before, a neat hole cut in the fence, leading to a little hill. *Yemaya* wrecked most of the trees, but I can see the remnants of the bench and the little library. *Infinite Jest* lays in the mud, ripped in half down the spine. That's what you get, David Foster Wallace. There's no sign of Althea. I hope she's okay.

"Ben and I pooled the money we made and printed business cards saying, 'Reduce your sentence with Jackson and Hughes, Counselors-at-Law,' and the number of a pay phone in a barber shop." Jackson finishes.

"Ben took in enough fees to pay his tuition." Jackson laughs long and free, and the sound echoes along the river, rattling the leaves hiding the cicadas that wait for us to pass so they can restart the world. "You know, I never ran tables again."

"Tight jeans, you make this shit up?" the jogger asks.

Jackson doesn't reply. Instead, he unties his Africa medallion, looks at it for a moment, and then holds it out to me. I can't think of what to say. I reach out and take the medallion.

My head separates from the hull. I gently fall to earth. The ground feels real and normal under my feet. My body still aches, but the pain feels far off, like a thunderstorm in the next county.

Adrian lets go of *Yemaya*, but stays aloft, floating a few inches above the flowers that spring up in her wake. She drifts across the ground. I only now realize she's barefoot.

The jogger slowly separates from the ship, drifting closer and closer to the ground until she lands lightly. Frost spreads under her feet. I can't help but notice the way she looks at Jackson. The way every woman looks at Jackson, but more.

Cicadas restart the world. Chirps fill the silent spaces. The sun begins to rise, a rim of yellow across a dark horizon. Birds chirp, but the Cheeper-Cheeper Tape bird has nothing to say yet. *Yemaya* looms over us, quieter than before.

I've thought of what to say. If the past isn't set or fixed but just a collection of stories like Cut Mary says, then Jackson just created an alternate timeline with new possibilities. I do not have to be me. I can write myself into a new space and time, new possibilities, new relationships. Every word, every conversation, every decision creates and recreates my life. I can start a revolution, or stop one, or write a book, read a book, anything. I do not stand on the hub of the world. I am the hub of the world. I am the Cicada Clock.

Jackson stands lightly with the ship balanced perfectly on his head. I turn to thank my best friend and BOOM! A bullet bursts through Jackson's chest and flings his blood across my face.

After a tragedy, there's always a sense of unfairness, of feeling betrayed, of wondering why the world keeps spinning and the sun keeps shining like they don't care, like whatever created us moved off long ago and left us to figure things out for ourselves and make whatever plan we think works. A feeling that we've passed through a door that locked behind us without warning and now, now we're more alone than before.

"Gimme your hands! Right now, goddammit!" men yell.

Adrian screams, "Jackson! Jackson!" She flies to him.

Yemaya slips from his head and rests on the back of his neck. The weight of the ship presses down on him. Adrian clamps her hand to the gushing wound in his chest but there's too much blood and all I can think is, it's too late, too late. The jogger stands frozen in place.

I don't care if *Yemaya* crushes more trees, or falls and kills us all. My friend is, is—and I have to help, to be there, to do something.

Ethiopia Jackson grins at us.

I get under the ship and try to lift it, pushing and straining until I feel every muscle strain under the pressure. I might as well move a mountain. "Help me!" I yell. No one else moves.

"Hands up—can't run—gotcha now," the men yell again. Only Jackson moves, putting his hands up to steady the ship. I want to tell him don't worry about the ship now but, Jackson. It's impossible. Jackson can't die.

"Jackson!" Adrian wails.

Yemaya rocks to one side and bumps a tree. Suddenly, birds flee the ruckus in a dark noisy cloud overhead.

"I said—put your hands up right—goddamn now!" Wending Strickland points a rifle at my face. Behind him stand Mending and Pats, plus a scattering of my former neighbors. Blood pumps from Ethiopia's chest through Adrian's fingers.

"My hands are up," I shout.

"He's dying!" Adrian says.

"All hell done broke loose—still running around loose— looser than a two dollar whore on dollar day," say Pats and the Stricklands.

The cicadas whirr like today is any other day.

"Why did you shoot him?" I ask.

"He didn't—obey my—lawful order," Pats and the Stricklands say.

"Put me on a t-shirt," Ethiopia says.

"Since when are you cops?" Adrian asks. Even now, she's still floating above the ground. I hope they don't notice.

"Destroyed my property! —My trees! —My house! — Destroy your own house—nigger—don't destroy mine."

"You shot me for a tree? A tree?" Ethiopia Jackson laughs loud, long, black, deep. "A tree!" His laughter runs loose across The Through and I see shimmering people again, getting haircuts and going to school, leaning over fences, chasing kids. Jackson keeps laughing, and every sound fills in colors and light and Randolph's voice comes back, clear as the day we stood in the street drinking beer and he said, "Okahika, my home."

Jackson bleeds and bleeds. His blood runs down his shirt and onto the ground in a single snaky tendril. The tendril side-winds across the ground towards Mending Strickland. Mending's legs quiver but he doesn't move. The blood curls upwards, around his leg, past his waist, over his arms and hands and gun.

The jogger glares at Pats and the Stricklands. "Get out," she spits. "Get the fuck out before I hurt you. Go home."

"Go," Jackson says, "Go home."

Ethiopia Jackson.

Adrian runs her hands over his chest uselessly. "Jackson, I'm so sorry," she says.

"*Yemaya*," he replies. "Good name."

Ethiopia Jackson.

"Go home Ben Hotep," he says, "Go home." With his last breath, he heaves *Yemaya* upwards, just a little, just enough that I feel the weight of her lift from my spine. The weight drives his knee to the ground. Every muscle strains. He lets his head droop sideways and then stops, arms still outstretched, holding *Yemaya* aloft. The blood tendril falls to the ground like normal blood.

I grab Ethiopia's shoulder. He's cold, smooth as carved marble. His face looks resigned, peaceful. That deep, subterranean current pushed us here, but left him high and dry. I don't know what to do. There's nothing I can do. Go home, he said. I don't have a home. No story can reinvent a bullet in the chest. My perspective doesn't matter, my past doesn't matter, nothing matters.

Adrian places her hands around Jackson's face. One hand bleeds. She murmurs something I can't make out. A prayer, maybe. The jogger radiates chilly cold.

BOOM. The gun goes off again.

"Adrian?" I say. Her eyes are wide.

"Adrian?" I scream. The jogger runs to her twin. We touch her everywhere, frantic.

"I'm fine," she says. "I'm fine."

"Ow! —You shot me—Why'd you shoot me?" Pats and the Stricklands say. They've shot Mending in the foot.

BOOM! They shoot Pats in the foot.

"I can't let the damn gun loose—give it here—Just let it go—"

BOOM! They shoot Wending in the foot.

"Well shit—all that one's fault—we gots to sue," they say. "Us," they say, pointing at themselves, "you," they say, pointing at each other, "them," they say, pointing at our neighbors. "We all gonna—get together—class action—we gone get certified—take every penny."

Ha! I think. I'm broke. You can't rob a man who has nothing. When I'd imagined myself in the Subaru and the tweed, listening to NPR, I still thought college professor—professoring? professing—was a noble job. A big deal. Proof I'd made it. With my brains, not my looks. But the job changed. No one came to me and said, 'Adjuncting is a dead-end job. Are you cool with that?' but I knew it the day I signed on. I saw it in the way the real faculty couldn't quite look me in the eye, or fidgeted, or pursed their lips, just before the Chair announced additional work for no pay. I knew it in the way I did more work for no pay, even though I bitched and moaned about it the whole time, I still did the work while wondering if I'd have enough to keep the lights on all month. Deep down, I preferred going nowhere instead of always scanning the horizon, so to speak, to see what was coming next. I stayed in my little cave and only peeked out when someone called for me. Nothing took me here. Nothing will take me home.

I take a step backwards. Sunlight, bright and yellow, lights my back, but the jogger's cold fury prevents any heat from reaching me. Dark clouds gather. Our neighbors stand horrified. Pats and the Stricklands limp around like Civil War re-enactors and argue over who's the lead plaintiff. Their breath makes small clouds that linger over their heads. I take another step. The cicadas get louder. Adrian takes my hand and I pull her with me. No one seems to notice us. The opening in the fence brushes my shoulder. *Yemaya* lifts off Jackson's shoulders and begins to float away. Light peeks through the hole in his back and chest, but his flesh has become black marble, onyx, the densest granite, immovable.

The jogger shakes. She sputters, "I loved him!" She screams, and the ground shakes. Thunderclouds deluge us in a cold rain. The water begins to cover my feet. "I loved him!" The river rises and demolishes the levee with a thundering roar, sweeping debris and water towards us in a furious wave. Our neighbors run. Pats and the Stricklands limp away, but the water sweeps them off their feet. They cling to each other and go under.

The jogger screams without words. Water falls from the hull, drenching us to the bone. Her body melts, as fragile as Jackson's body is solid. She bleeds water. Her arm falls off, then her head. Her torso splits in half and each leg crumbles. In the rushing water, I see the stump of one foot, still frozen to the ground. The rest vanishes into the flood.

"Noooooo!" Adrian wails. "No, no, no, no!"

The water rises above my waist, then up to my neck. I'm frozen in place. I'm going to drown. I'm going to die. There's nowhere to go. I have no home. I thrash uselessly. Tomorrow, the sun will come up, cicadas will sing, and the world will tick its time away without me.

I push Adrian away frantically. She can't die here, not like this. "Go, go," I shout over the pounding rain. "Fly! Get out of here."

"Come on!" Adrian yells back. The water covers my eyes. Adrian reaches down and takes my hand with hers. Pain shoots through us, violent, savage. I slip under.

B E N

You,
Ben Hotep

Did I turn the stove off before *Yemaya* destroyed the house?
Ships? I'll never hear the end of it. Blood from a gash on my
calf slithers off into the weeds. I stomped on the ground three
times. I hit myself in the head to get water out of my ear. I
have one good eye. I peel the black skin from a butterpear and
eat the creamy green flesh. Yes, we have no butt-er-pears, we
have no butt-er-pears today. I walk though deep ruts in a curvy
mud road. I jump up the concrete stairs to my house, open
the screen door so hard I break the frame, sit on the couch,
and open a copy of a men's exercise magazine with Ethiopia
Jackson's byline. 'Chopped Arms, Ripped Chest.' The snake
from *Roots* crawls out of my first edition copy (bought in the
clearance bin) and suns itself on the porch. Families walk by
the window, laughing and taking photos, never seeing me see

them, never seeing the snake coiled to strike. The oven clock reads 8:23 a.m. My watch says 9:15 AM. The man on the TV says Noon. A rooster cockfights the Cheeper-Cheeper Tape bird. Cicadas rewind the clock and people move talk walk backwards. Randolph drives a rusty tractor backwards ran into an old tree with blue glass stuck in the branches. Sparks fly. Randolph jumps off the tractor and runs forwards. Cut Mary pulls herself out of the tree and stands in the sunlight. I had to tell her something. I had to tell her something. I read 'Chopped Arms, Ripped Chest' again. Adrian walks out of the bedroom wearing an old t-shirt. Adrian unwraps the bandage on her hand and shows me long scars across her palm, an X design with numbers and letters. I shrink. The room grows. My feet touch the floor. My feet dangle in mid-air. This doesn't make sense. Things should make sense. This doesn't make sense. Things should make sense. I bite my tongue. The cockfight spills onto the porch. The snake calls time out. The rooster walks away. The Cheeper-Cheeper Tape Bird flies away. Adrian drops her bloody bandage on the floor and walks into air, across the porch, over the fight, into the front yard and plucks a peach from the tree we thought would never grow. 'I love you,' I should have said. I should have said that every day since we met. "I know," she says, and walks off eating a peach with her good hand. I sip coffee on our too-large couch. I shrink until my feet come off the floor, then grow back to normal size, except for my head, which keeps growing and growing until it bursts through the roof, startling the Cheeper-Cheeper Tape

Bird, stopping it from eating cicadas and forever silencing the clock of the world. My soft bones need calcium. I try to go to the store and buy vitamins but my giant head holds me in place. I sit to read 'Chopped Arms, Ripped Chest' again, but my giant head holds me in place. My feet dangle. I raise my hands to my head like the Crazy Glue man, but my short arms only reach my chin. Crazy-Glue should hire me. Two themes of clayness sing an alternating song. My chest is red clay. My chin and knees, my ass and my calves are also made of red clay. My neck, arms and thighs are columns of red clay. My red clay jaw grinds words in my clay teeth. My tiny clay fingers massaged my clay jaw until some of the words dislodged, fell down my clay throat, and landed in my clay feet. Place words in my head and I will perform menial labor, I will write love stories, I will babysit college students, I will do whatever I'm supposed to do. Place words in my feet and I'll do the same. Cicadas burrow into my feet and eat my words. I don't have nerves, I'm clay, I feel nothing, but this hurt in a good way, like pulling knives from my feet after stabbing myself. I would never do that. 'Hey cicadas, that's not your job, don't do that, leave the knives in there, leave me alone, help, help,' they're taking the words I should have said. Maybe that is their job. If I don't release the words, they come along and release them for me, for everyone, every 13 years on the clock. Thank you cicadas. I shrink and shrink as the cicadas eat words from my feet. Bits of paper litter the floor. I bite my tongue. I shake litter from my feet. If I disappear, like the scene in *Brazil* when paperwork kills Robert DeNiro, no one will sort the trash looking for me. The Cheeper-Cheeper Tape Bird, covered in rooster blood, attacks the cicadas. GET TO WORK! it squawks. LAZY LUMPS! it squawks. CHEEPER-CHEEPER TAPE! it squawks. The cicadas scatter and leave me lumpen, unfinished.

"Took you long enough."

I opened my eyes and saw a wide circle of small houses on short stilts. Each house looked old and handmade. The steps and windows had all been shaped by hand, one at a time. Even the lumber looked hand-cut. I turned in a slow semi-circle and saw other buildings—barns, sheds, more houses large and small, surrounded by dark fields, but the whole place seemed centered around the circle of houses, which seemed centered around the fountain.

Bright sunlight shone overhead. Overhead? I looked up, but *Yemaya* wasn't there. She sat on Jackson's back. But he wasn't there either.

I looked down and saw that I stood in a low fountain made from flagstones, with a long column in the center. Water gurgled out of the center column and ran into the basin. I was filthy, covered in mud, sweat, and blood. Not my blood. My eyes felt sticky and hot from crying, but I didn't remember crying. My shirt dangled off to one side in shreds. Scratches covered my legs. My feet bloodied the water. A short piece of white gauze, stained into a rust color the water could not dissolve, floated by. I felt misshapen from the words the cicadas left behind.

"Step out of the water son. Let me take a look at you." I turned around. Cut Mary stood there, tall and substantial.

I was terrified. I always considered phrases like 'Anything is possible,' trite trash, but what if anything really was possible? Cut Mary could have been a ghost or a phantom or I was crazy and the Stricklands had every reason to shoot a mad dog lunatic walking the streets hallucinating ships and old women and Adrian no one was my friend no one loves me I had no home and Cut Mary touched my arm. My head shrank back to normal size. I stepped over the low rim of the fountain and sat down heavily. Cut Mary moved closer and held me closely. We stayed like that for a minute, and hour, a year, I'm not sure.

"I'm sorry about Jackson," I said.

"Yes, I know," she said, and I couldn't help the feeling that she did know, about the ship, The Through, the cicadas and the Cheeper-Cheeper Tape Bird, all of it. "I'm sorry about your relationship. You two had potential."

I looked up. "Wait. You mean, Adrian and I are, I mean we're—"

"You keep losing track of each other," Cut Mary said.

"We got separated," I said. "She held my hand and then, I don't know how to describe what happened next, but then I wound up here and she's gone."

"Separated?" Cut Mary asked. "Why did you do that?"

"Do what? Make a ship crash into our house?"

"If you two didn't make it happen, who did?" Cut Mary asked.

I stood shaking, furious. "I didn't make a flying ship or an ice woman. I wanted a normal day—"

"You start every day running in circles," Cut Mary said. "Up the jogging path, take a right down a side street, take a right down Fifth Avenue, take another right on Main Street and you're back where you started. Now you've changed course. You're running a different way, but it's not your fault? None of your doing? You're just an innocent bystander?"

I sat down again.

"I told y'all to plant that althea and comfrey. Did you?" Cut Mary asked.

"Adrian started but…no," I answered.

"Doing nothing is doing something. Well, that would have bought you a day at least. Then you could have come back and heard the rest together. Now I'll tell you, and you'll have to convince her on your own time."

Convince her of what?

"I admit," she said, stretching, "Feels good to be out and about again."

"I saw you climb out of a tree," I said. "I saw Randolph drive into a tree and you climb out," I said.

"Did you?" Cut Mary said. She narrowed her eyes. "Did you now? Huh. Randolph and I go way back. But our story doesn't directly help y'all not in any way I can think. You need to focus on your particular circumstances. Do you know where we are?"

I looked around. Twelve rickety houses on stilts surrounded the circular flagstone fountain. A curving road circled around the town in a spiral, ending at the fountain. Past the houses, I saw the same buildings, barns and sheds I'd seen before, under towering trees with hanging moss. A light fog clung to the ground. What could have been a church leaned against a stand of trees, and the front of one house had a large porch with chairs and a table. The occupants had placed an old-timey soda machine on the porch, the kind with a glass door. No people or animals, no sounds besides the tinkling water and our own voices. I didn't recognize a single landmark. I couldn't see the sun. The light diffused through low clouds. It could have been early morning, or midday, or evening.

"We're not in Northport," I said. "Not in The Through."

"Remember what Randolph called it?" Cut Mary asked.

I thought for a second. "Okahika. Jackson called it Okahika too. We can't be there. The Through doesn't look anything like this. No place in Northport looks like this."

"We're not in Northport," Cut Mary said.

"How can we not be in Northport?" I asked. My mouth felt salty and dry.

"Because we're in Okahika," Cut Mary said, like it was perfectly obvious.

"That's impossible," I said.

"Possible," Cut Mary said, smiling. "Possible." Cut Mary stood and walked towards the dusty general store. "I'm getting a drink. Want something?"

I needed something, anything to drink. Idiot, I thought. I'm standing in a fountain. The blood and mud on my clothes turned the basin water pink, but the flowing water looked cool and clear. I leaned over and took a sip, then immediately spat it out. Saltwater. What was it with me and saltwater?

"Coming, or you gonna try drinking that?" Cut Mary asked. She had already crossed to the store and walked up the rickety stairs.

I climbed out of the fountain and hurried across the road to catch up. As I drew closer, I saw the outlines of signs on the front wall of the store. The porch itself was larger than I expected, not just a space to get out of the weather, but a place to visit with neighbors. Poles made from tree trunks held up the roof, and carefully stacked rocks supported the floor. Under years of dust, old wooden signs advertised W.E. Garrett and Sons, Gulf Oil, Chesterfield Cigarettes, and other companies long gone out of business. A sign over the door had rusted away, but the first two letters looked like J and A. The furniture—a table, a few chairs—looked handmade. I sat down on a rocking chair missing a runner.

Cut Mary peered into the soda machine. "Looks like grape or peach."

Old, hot soda had to be better than saltwater. "Peach, please," I said.

"Peach," Cut Mary said, then pulled a blissfully cold peach Nehi soda from the machine. She handed it to me. "And a grape," she said before pulling another bottle out.

Cut Mary sat next to me at the dusty table, put the bottle in her mouth, pried the cap off with her teeth, and took a long sip. She set it down, and just then I noticed a checkerboard design painted onto the tabletop, covered in dust just like everything else.

"I'll tell you something might could explain," she said. "Or not. Up to you." She drank again.

I'd never felt thirst like that, like my throat had turned to salt and gravel. I considered putting the bottle in my teeth and taking my chances.

"We're in Okahika, Florida," Cut Mary said. "What's left of it. Most people left this place years ago. You've already been to Okahika, Alabama, but you call it The Through. Adrian's grandparents lived in Okahika, Louisiana. And you've been to my house. I live on the edge of town, right where the trees start." She pointed off to the left. Through the mist and the hanging moss I saw a house with dark windows. Were those blue windows? I couldn't tell from the porch.

"Okay. Different towns with the same name," I said, still looking through the trees. "But how did we get to Florida? A drive to Florida would take five or six hours." No way I'd been out that long. Unless she drugged me. That could explain everything. Maybe this whole thing resulted from a drug trip. But I already knew. Whatever the explanation, drugs weren't it. Plausible, yes, but too easy. Whatever happened took more than a pill.

"Okahika lives in a bunch of states—Georgia, the Carolinas, Mississippi, Tennessee, Kentucky, Arkansas, Louisiana. Even Texas. Might be one or two others out there. Never had time to visit all of them, but all Okahikas occupy the same place. Surprised you picked Florida. Had to follow in a rush."

"You didn't bring me here?" I asked.

"You ain't heard me. You chose the direction."

"I didn't. I just—I don't know how I got here."

"I told you, all Okahikas occupy the same place. If you ain't careful, you can enter Okahika in one place and leave from another." She took another sip. "You ain't careful."

This made no sense. "Look, I need answers," I said. "Did you drive us here? You have a car tucked away in one of these barns?"

Cut Mary sighed. "You gonna drink that or what?" she asked.

The unopened bottle felt cold, solid, real. I needed a drink badly.

"There's no bottle opener," I said.

Cut Mary took the bottle from my hand, opened it with her teeth, spat out the cap, and handed the bottle back. I couldn't think of what to do but drink. The soda flowed straight up my nose.

Cut Mary laughed. "Them little ten-ounce bottles are tricky," she said. "Hold your mouth open when you drink. Wider. That's it."

The soda tasted like magic. I never had a drink that tasted so good before. I drank half the bottle in one go.

"Drink up," Cut Mary said. "Plenty more where these came from."

"Thank you," I said, "but can you tell me what's happening here? Adrian, Jackson, the ship, the jogger, how I supposedly got to Florida?"

"Supposedly?"

"It would take hours to drive to Florida. There's no way I was out for that long."

"Where's Marcel?" Cut Mary asked.

I'd completely forgotten about him. "Last I saw, he was walking in front of us. Did he drive? Is that what happened?"

"You arrived on your own two feet. I keep telling you."

"Mother Jackson—"

"My name ain't Jackson and I never had kids."

"Cut Mary, I just want the facts. Just tell me what's really going on here."

"You need truth, not facts."

"Same thing," I said.

Cut Mary looked at me over her glasses. "This might take longer than I thought. Come on, we gotta make room." Cut Mary stood. "Getting late. Folks coming to talk. Let's get inside."

I looked around. Nothing had changed. The streets were empty. The fountain tinkled in the distance. No birds, no cicadas, no animals at all. The light shined the same as it did when I arrived, diffuse and directionless. I couldn't tell if we'd been there for minutes or hours.

"Or," Cut Mary said, "You can take that road." She pointed at one of the curving roads leading to the fountain in the center of town. "Follow the road and you'll find your old job, your wrecked house, all that shit you worry about so much."

"Will I find Adrian?"

"You've lived with Adrian for years and not found her. Think a road will make a difference?"

Cut Mary got up and walked inside. She moved slowly and intentionally, like each step had to be placed exactly there and no other place in the universe. Like if she tripped or stumbled, there would be consequences. The screen door slapped shut. I looked around. Everything still looked the same. I finished my soda, and followed Cut Mary into the store. I didn't have a lot of options.

Inside, Cut Mary set one grape and one peach soda on a small table facing the window that opened to the porch. I looked out and saw the porch just as I found it - the broken chairs, the checkerboard, and everything covered in dust. I turned to brush the dust off my legs before I sat, but there didn't seem to be any dust on me. As a matter of fact, my bleeding leg didn't leave any mark on the porch - no stains, no drops. My swollen eye worked. The water that soaked my shoes disappeared. I looked outside again. Everything on the porch looked exactly as I'd first seen it. Not one mote of dust moved. We left no footprints, as if the place existed, but we didn't.

I felt my chest. Nothing. I grabbed at me wrist, my neck, anywhere with a pulse. Nothing.

Cut Mary dragged another handmade chair to the table. "Sit down," she said.

"Are we dead?" I asked.

"Dead? Who said anything about being dead?" Cut Mary said. "Sit down. If you sit, you might start to understand. And drink your soda."

The dust lifted like dense fog, revealing a well-built, well cared for store at the center of a lively small town. Colored street lamps hung from trees outside, illuminating men and women walking to the store in couples or small groups. Inside, a lanky man in the corner played guitar blues and a woman in a red dress sang. *"I got nipples on my titties, big as the end of my thumb. I got somethin between my legs, that'll make a dead man cum."* Everyone laughed.

Several women gathered on the porch. Most of them looked about Cut Mary's age, or her era if not exactly her age. Some younger, some older, but from the same time. They all had her look, like where they stepped mattered and what they did mattered. I'd never been in a place like this before. A man, perhaps a husband, leaned against a pillar. A preacher, judging by his suit, fanned himself with his hat. They began speaking. Everyone spoke at once, cutting into each other's words. I caught snippets of stories. A man had been lynched and lived to tell about it. In fact, he wouldn't shut up about it. Cats held a funeral parade. A woman searched the fields for the heart of her dead lover hidden in a daisy. A couple scandalized an entire town when he went down on her while everyone watched through the windows. An old man carried kerosene. A sea captain drowned while Africans flew. Newborn babies spoke. On and on, story after story woven together, some funny, some sad, some sexual, some brutal, but all of them fascinating, all of them true.

The woman in the corner sang a new song, something about flagging a ride and sinking down. I couldn't concentrate. Cut Mary filled her house with plants. Was one of them an abnormally large daisy with a heart inside it? Felt like I'd visited her years ago. I turned and looked at her, really looked at her, for the first time. Cut Mary appeared to be in her mid-60's, short, with dreadlocks turned silvery-white with black tips. Her broad brown forehead showed few wrinkles. If anything, her face looked like she'd suppressed a laugh for most of her life, some secret joy known to her alone. She wore a simple strand of white beads around her neck, but no other jewelry. She wore a long blue and white dress, partially covered with a green sweater.

Seeing the sweater brought me back to my own body, shivering in the cold. Had the weather changed while I listened to those stories? The people on the porch spoke as if these events had happened when they were kids. No, as if they'd heard these stories as children, but the actual events took place long before.

Where is Okahika? When is Okahika?

"How's that book of yours coming?" Cut Mary asked.

Every writer hates that question. Every writer who hasn't written a thing in years especially hates that question. "It's not, really," I said.

"Why's that?" Cut Mary asked.

"Wait a minute," I said. "That story, the one about the daisy, was that about you?"

"Tell you what," she said, "you answer one question and I'll answer one. Does that make sense?"

"Yes, okay, yes."

"So why can't you write your book?"

Why can't I write my book? "I'm a hack, an imitator with no real talent, a joke, a nice guy who hangs out with writers but can't put it together, lazy. I have nothing significant to say." All the words tumbled out before I could stop them, but only Cut Mary seemed to hear. The residents of Okahika played cards and dominoes, drank, sang, danced, made jokes and laughed, told old stories, kissed, lived. Hearing me might have bored them to death.

"You can ask me a question," Cut Mary said, smiling. "Even though you never answered mine."

"Whoa," I said, "I told you. I've never told anyone that. Not even Adrian."

"You got a question in all that self-doubt?"

My bottom lip quivered for no reason. "Where's Adrian? Is she okay?"

"Two questions. Well since you're a nice boy, I'll answer both. Adrian's in Okahika, but not this Okahika. And no, she's not okay. She has a tough path ahead. She's going to need help."

"Where? Where is she? How can she be here and not here? How do I get to her?" I asked.

"More questions. I gave you a freebie before, but that's enough. Time for you to answer my question. But maybe you're not ready. I'll ask an easier question: what's the difference between facts and truth?"

Facts and truth? "You asked before, didn't you? Same thing."

"Wrong. Try again."

"Fact and truth are synonyms, or close enough," I insist. "There's no real difference."

"If I were to tell you facts are the observable world around us, what facts can you tell me about Okahika? Look around."

The store. The circle of houses and the fountain, which now, come to think of it, didn't really make sense here. Two curved roads intersecting. The farms beyond the houses. The store, the old signs. I felt it, I touched it, I heard the music and the laughter. I told Cut Mary all of this and unexpectedly, she agreed.

"We're settled on the facts then. But truth is a different animal. Facts concern what we can see, but truth concerns what we can't see. Truth is wisdom, Ben, guidance. Truth helps us make decisions when the facts don't point one way or another. So why can't you write, Ben Hotep?"

I took a long breath and closed my eyes. I felt the answer in my gut. If I let it out I wasn't sure what would happen. If I deflected her, she would return to this again and again. I didn't have another answer to give.

"I can't write," I said, "because there's something wrong with me. I can't seem to figure my life out. I go to the store and see couples walking around happy, having kids. My coworkers tell me about stuff they do on the weekends, but they never invite me. Their parents, their families do normal things together but I never get that. Adrian and I don't do stuff couples do. My whole life is off-kilter. It's like I missed the one little thing everyone else figured out a long time ago." I hung my head. "Something's wrong with me, and everyone knows it, but no one will tell me what it is. There, I said it. I feel like a fool but I said it."

"So that's what's been bugging you this whole time. And now I suppose you want me to tell you the answer?"

I looked up. "Wait. You know? Please tell me. Whatever it is, I don't care."

"Hate," she said, "can work wonders. Hate gives power. Hate lets you turn off your instinct for self-preservation if it means defeating your enemy. But hate comes with a high price. Hate cost the life of someone I loved once."

"I don't hate anyone," I said.

"Sure you do. Someone you're so busy hating that you don't listen to Adrian, don't see her. You never gather her facts, so you can't understand her truth."

"Who!" I demanded. "Who is it?"

"To her, it don't look like hate. It looks like love. She thinks you're so absorbed with someone else."

"Who is it?" I screamed.

"You, Ben Hotep. It's you."

Music played. People talked and laughed and drank beer and gin. Couples found little spaces just large enough to hide two sweaty bodies. I sat in a pool of my own misery, looking at nothing in particular. *You, Ben Hotep.* I did this to myself. I'd been so obsessed with myself I'd never made room for anyone else.

My whole life flashed before my eyes, but not from my perspective. I saw what I looked like to others, how I treated everyone else. A lonely, isolated child, pushing friends away, skipping birthday parties and proms. Ungrateful, unforgiving, selfish when my mother made dinner and I wanted something different or refused to eat. The hurt in her eyes was clear in my memory. Why hadn't I seen it before? *You, Ben Hotep.* That ridiculous fight I started in college over medallions, of all things, but people got hurt and wound up with records because of me. And Adrian. I let Adrian into my house, but not into myself. When I saw her twin, a version of Adrian without her pain, I couldn't even recognize her. Adrian, wherever you are, I'm sorry. I'm sorry for everything. I'm sorry for being me. I'm sorry for not sorting myself out before you came. I'm sorry for all the things I never said and didn't do. I'm sorry for being Ben Hotep instead of Ben Hughes. I don't even know Ben Hughes.

Cut Mary put her hands on my shoulders. I hadn't realized I'd been rocking myself back and forth, speaking my thoughts aloud. "Ben, I don't know what your one little thing is. But you have to release this self-hatred before you can find it. Otherwise, hate will drag you down like a drowning horse."

I don't know how. "I don't know how."

"I can see that," she said, but not unkindly. "And the truth is, you'll have to sort it out for yourself. Here's what I can do for you right now: I can tell you more about Okahika, about how you got in and how to leave, if that's what you want. I can tell you where Adrian is, if you want to go to her. And I can get you another pop."

The singer took a break, and the guitarist sang his own song about drinking champagne and smoking dope. Everyone laughed and danced. I opened and closed my mouth a few times, then finally said, "D. All of the above." Dried mud flaked from my cheek and fell to the floor.

Cut Mary and I sipped sodas while the music played. "Okahika," Cut Mary said. "The names means 'the people by the cliff' and a few other things. Some say it was a Choctaw name, others said the Choctaw made up a new word for us, and some say we made up a word that just sounded like Choctaw. Can't tell you for sure. All I know is Okahika was Okahika is Okahika will be Okahika. You and Adrian saw a little piece of it, when you came to my house. But you'd seen Okahika already. Shimmers of people living lives, old signs pointing out what used to be, places where things don't quite add up. Spot a bottletree, that's a signpost. Listen to the cicadas, they'll sing you home."

"I've heard a lot of cicadas lately."

"They're as good a path as any," Cut Mary says. She finishes her grape soda and opens another. "Every Southern state has an Okahika. A few states have more than one. Some got people living there still, others are abandoned, some got burnt to the ground and rebuilt. It's the path that brings us here. Not the road, the path. A strangeness, a wanting to know, a juke joint rhythm."

"Adrian and I entered in Alabama," I said. "I came out here, in Florida."

"Something like that."

"So which Okahika did Adrian go to?"

"Ben, you need to hear me. Every Okahika is the same Okahika and completely different."

"That doesn't make—" I stopped. "So you're saying this Okahika is the same location as The Through?"

"Fact and truth together."

"But when I leave, I could wind up anywhere. Any Southern state, you said."

"That's right."

"And Adrian is here?"

"Everyone is somewhere," Cut Mary said. "Your heart could guide you to her, but I don't think you're learned to read what's in there, and you definitely ain't learned to read hers. What you need young man, is a good map and some transportation." She looked up, over my head.

"Oh no. No. Not *Yemaya*," I said.

"She was trying to bring you here, but you ran every which way but the way you were supposed to go."

"She destroyed my house and half of downtown! She nearly broke my back! The only reason I'm here at all is Jackson." Trapped under *Yemaya* forever.

"He walked his own path and got where he was going. Don't blame yourself. Your path, on the other hand, is yet to be determined."

A deafening crack shook the building and knocked all the dancers to the floor. A thick hemp rope dropped in front of my face.

"Adrian got her own map. It wrote itself on her hand. You saw it, but you didn't really see it."

"The cuts," I said. "She said she was fine."

"Trust me, she's not fine, but she's going where she needs to go. She'll need your help, Ben, but listen good. She needs your unvarnished attention. She needs you to set your ego to the side. Do that, and you might be able to help her. I'm not saying you will or won't. You have a chance. That's all I can offer. But you gotta choose. Up or out Ben," Cut Mary said. "Pick a path."

I looked as far as I could down the road leading out of town. If I started walking now, I might find a hotel before dark. At the very least, I could flag down a passing driver and catch a ride to a gas station. I'd find a way home, and then go back to my old job. I could sleep in my office while the house was repaired. If anyone asked about the crazy events and the storm, I'd say I had amnesia and couldn't tell them anything. People would talk for a while, and then football season would roll around again and everyone would forget about me, and I would forget about myself, just like always. Just like always.

I put my hand around the rope without touching it. Sharp hemp splinters shot out in every direction. Whatever happened next would hurt. I took a deep breath and grabbed the rough rope.

Cut Mary smiled at me. "Good choice," she said.

I ran to Cut Mary and wrapped her in a tight hug. "Thank you," I said. "Thank you."

Cut Mary returned the hug with real affection. After a minute, she pushed me away and wiped a tear from her eye. She said, "Let me give you a bit of advice."

I nodded.

"That man you love and hate so much? Cut him a little slack. You might finish that book you're so worried about." Cut Mary told me. "Plenty of good stories in Okahika, if you get stuck."

I smiled, my first real, honest smile in a long time. "I'm not worried about my book anymore," I said.

"Good," she said. "Now go. Get up that rope."

I turned, grabbed the rope, and climbed for a second or forever.

A D R I A N

Giving Birth and Eating the Sun

I am

        Filthy floodwater

            wind

       rain

       oceans and seas and rivers

                       amniotic

       blessed

       banished

            flowing into sand and out again.

"Ben, come on!" I yelled through the surging water. I took his good hand with mine, my crossed hand. Pain and heat shot through us both. I screamed until I stopped and arrived here, alone.

    I stood beside a mud-caked fence on a broken sidewalk after a tornado. Trash and debris lay everywhere, and water soaked the ground. Surrounding me, I saw about a dozen houses around a cul-de-sac, all wrecked. These places weren't modern homes, but more of the older style I saw growing up. This was a rough neighborhood. Their owners painted their homes in bright colors once, pink, red, gold, purple. Now black mold stained the walls, making the houses look like plague victims. Graffiti marked each door. Where was I? I looked around for clues, but every house on this street lay knocked off its foundation. Street signs had been torn off the poles. Some trees lay broken on their sides or completely uprooted. Cars poked out of their branches.

"Ben!?" I called. "Ben?" No answer. Had he come with me? I don't want to remember. My hand throbbed. I'd lost my bandage somewhere in the flood. My sister, the flood. My sister, the flood, who drowned Ben and most of our town after they shot Jackson. Jackson. In a flash, I saw the life we could have had and the senselessness of his death, the horror, overcame me. I wailed like a lost thing.

Everyone I love dies. Ben wants me to love him the way he loves me but everyone I love dies before their time. The only way I can love him is to keep him at arm's length. My love is fatal.

The nappy-headed doll lay sprawled out on the sidewalk, face up, eyes fixed at the sky. A Winn-Dixie calendar lay a few feet over. From another door, a young man emerged, kissed his wife and baby goodbye, and got into his car, never noticing that his house tilted to one side and his car sat in a tree. Several old men sat in front of a small store and drank from bottles hidden in paper bags. A girl walked by, careful to avoid the drunks. She must have been coming home from school, judging by her uniform. Across the road, a large woman threw her belongings into her car. She might have been 35 or 40. She ran back inside to get something else. After a few minutes, she emerged with her purse and a small dog. A man ran out of the house after her. He didn't want her to leave. No, he didn't want the dog to leave. He snatched the leash from her hands. They argued, and then she pulled a gun from her purse and pointed it at his head. Then the scene repeated. I saw the nappy-headed doll on the sidewalk, the calendar, the young man with his family, the drunks and the little girl, and the couple arguing over their dog, again, all again in an endless loop. Would they ever get anywhere? I couldn't look away at first, but I couldn't help them. I couldn't help anyone. I forced myself to focus on the doll.

Water had wiped all the features from her face and bloated her body. My sister died trying to save her from the flood. My sister is alive. Someone had written on the calendar in purple highlighter. August 29 must have been a special day. The note, like her face, was too smeared to read. With nothing else to do, I started to cover her face with the calendar. Everyone needs some kind of dignity, even nappy-headed dolls.

The calendar changed size in my hand, or the doll changed size on the sidewalk. Her arms and legs grew longer. Her torso thickened, and her head grew to human size. Her skin still looked waxy and dirty.

She opened her eyes and asked, "Ain't you raised better?"

"Yes ma'am," I said.

"Now I got ink all over my face. Turn it over so you don't ruin my makeup."

I started to tell her that her polyester dress stank, and that the flood washed off her makeup and her eyes, nose, and lips with it. She was probably cooking plastic food or watching her little plastic TV when it happened. Bits of the family Nativity scene lay scattered on the sidewalk next to her. I gathered up ceramic sheep and Joseph's bottom half. "Was he your husband?" I asked. "You should have taken cover."

"You should have taken cover," she replied.

Parts of ceramic people littered the street: Mary, the Three Wise Men, a shepherd. I pushed the ceramic bits into a pile on the sidewalk. Sheep and cattle, stuck together like conjoined twins. Joseph, broken in half. Mary swaddled in blue, her beautiful porcelain eyes cast down to the place where the Baby Jesus had lain amongst the animals. It was just a jagged hole now, but I could see where his little body had lay asleep in the hay. Baby Jesus' head floated in the gutter. I stared at his cherubic face, all rosy cheeks and blonde curls. Each piece called to me silently, wondering if I could just reach down and place Baby Jesus' ceramic head back on his ceramic body. I gathered all the pieces I could find and piled them next to the doll. Some child would come back someday and find her and the Nativity and know someone cared for them. Her people could put it all back together. I wondered what had happened to them. Their home, once so pretty and proud, the place where they gathered before parades and after church, the place they left and came back to because home is always home no matter how far you fly, their home vomited their lives into the gutter, their home no longer a resident, just another drunk tourist.

My hand bled. Blood dripped onto the ceramic pile and ran into a puddle. I knew I hadn't cut myself on the Nativity figurines. I knew that the way I knew a tornado didn't cause this damage and I wasn't in Northport. I didn't want to look, didn't want to look, but I looked at my hand. The symbols in each quadrant returned in small but painful red blisters: 8-29, O, 1-2, AD. I had nothing to wrap it with, so I pressed my hand to my chest. The pain came so sudden and shocking I fell to my knees. I should have fallen to my knees. I saw a flash of light, and my knees buckled. I fell into a bouquet of small flowers under me. My knees and feet never touched the ground. I can't say I was flying, but I wasn't walking, and written under me in blood red flowers was the Katrina Cross and I knew where I was. New Orleans. Home.

I see

      the crossroads
      the 24th letter
      the chi

         in Xmas.

     constant consonant constant

        Queen's English

      fertile earth

        the cliffside at the mountains west of town

    the trestle bridge crossing the river

In the hospital, they made me try to remember everything I forgot. What's your name? Tell us about your childhood? Where's your family? I never told them I remembered everything the whole time. I remembered too much. I remember too much. As a girl, everything seemed alive. The sunlight shone brighter. But after Marcel, the birds flew too close. Music thudding from cars made me put my hands over my ears and walk the other way. I began avoiding men, which Mama said made me stuck up and Marcel took for loyalty. "Yeah baby girl," he said. "Ain't no one for you but me." He was inside me when he said it, and I felt so proud of myself for being loyal, for attracting a grown man, for taking it, for learning all the things he wanted me to learn and doing all the things he liked, for keeping my mouth shut. I wore loyalty around like a badge. That's about when my twin told me that we loved Marcel and he loved us, he had to, because men and women didn't do what we did without loving each other. We were so in love. We would marry Marcel and have his babies. I might have been eleven or twelve.

I have almost no memory of the time between the birthday when Miss Janice gave me the book and when I turned 13, after Marcel quit me and in a fit of disloyal rage I told Mama everything. Everything. We'd been fighting. My grades had fallen from straight A's to D's and F's and she kept on me like she gave a shit about what I thought, like anything mattered anymore. I don't know exactly what I said, but everything spilled out of me—the times we snuck away, the times he came to my room, what happened under the banana tree, after school, before school, everything. I don't know what I expected. Anger maybe, or shock. I thought I'd have to defend Marcel from her. But I saw something else. Mama changed and I saw recognition in her eyes. "You knew?" I asked. "You knew the whole time?"

The most awful silence ever heard on Earth followed. Mama chewed her jaw. Finally, after a full minute, Mama said, "You are a lie."

I began shouting after that. I shouted at everyone. I shouted at church, at school, at home. I dated other boys and shouted when they fucked me. I shouted when they didn't fuck me. I shouted because I was shouting. The hospital didn't get me to remember, they got me to stop shouting.

Here, in this place, I took to shouting again. Nights only at first, then daytime too. I shouted for three days. "Hello! Someone say something!" No one spoke except the doll, and she only complained about her face. The scene repeated itself again: dead woman, calendar, family, girl, drunks, dog, gun. I moved to the other side of the street and watched them again. Nothing changed. Nothing else moved. No birds, no stray dogs or cats, not even a mosquito. I shouted again and again. Shouting took the edge off, made home seem a little less like a graveyard. The sun and moon rose and set.

"Say something," I muttered to little Lord Jesus' head, atop the pile of pottery. "Say something." Water dripped from cars and busted rooftops. "Say something!" I shouted. Nothing. I slapped the Nativity pile, driving sharp shards into my open palm. I didn't feel like paying attention to pain right now, so I set my hurt aside for later.

This was home wasn't it? New Orleans. But I didn't come here. I'd been somewhere else. People had been with me, but I didn't remember them. Why? I couldn't remember anything about leaving or coming back home. The idea unnerved me.

My hand bled again, but I had nothing clean to wrap it with. My yellow dress looked gray and frayed around the edges. Mud covered my legs up to the knees. I decided to explore the next house and see if I could find anything dry.

I pushed the swollen door open, scraping trash and a thick layer of mud from the floor. Inside, a long living room ran to a dining room and kitchen. A waterlogged couch blocked a side door. Green-black stains seeped into the plaster. And pictures of me. Me as a child in a plaid school uniform, me in church, me at a parade, me, me, me.

I gasped and fell backwards, then steadied myself on the door. A shrine. To me. Flowers, candles, the whole bit. I'd been kidnapped. Some kook had been stalking me. That explained everything. I'd overheard one of Ben's stupid podcasts once, about how often serial killers had Wayne as a middle name. His middle name probably was Wayne and he always seemed so nice, never made any trouble. "I ain't afraid of you," I shouted. "I ain't afraid of you, Wayne."

I picked up the first thing I could find, a heavy plate made of some pinkish clay with a red frog in the middle. I held it as high as I could in my good hand. Whoever had done this would not catch me sleeping. Who had done this? Who'd left me freezing and wet, cut up my hand? Probably some nut who thinks he got the spirit. "Ain't no spirit here," I shouted into the silence. Just you and me and this plate about to cave in your skull.

I will
        harm or heal
        mark the spot
        Name the long lost.
Put one foot in the grave and
        close
        the eyes of the dead

Mama went back to country ways just before she died. "It's the old ways m'dear," she used to say. I hated 'm'dear'. Mama never said 'm'dear' when I was a girl. Hearing her talk like that sounded like a foreigner had crawled into Mama's skin. "It's the old ways. This who we be," she said. Then came the candles and the flowers and all the crap. Communing with spirits. All bullshit. And this Wayne was bullshit, wherever he was, unless he was one of those who liked to fuck before getting sanctified. Or he could be one of the men outside, playing out the same scenes over and over. I checked myself quickly. He hadn't raped me yet, but something in my body wasn't right. Something deep had twisted or something twisted had gone deep. I searched the house room by room. I imagined blood spurting from his lice-ridden head, blood gushing from his neck. I'd kick him until his balls shot through his mouth. I'd gouge his eyes out and make him eat them and let wild animals tear his body apart.

"You gonna hurt somebody if you ain't mindful," a woman said. I whirled around and Cut Mary stood in the shrine like she owned it. I dropped the plate onto the floor. Cut Mary stepped gingerly over the wet trash. She looked like she did in her bottletree house, but smaller, as if walking around in the air diminished her, made her less Cut Mary than she was before.

"Too bad about the plate," Cut Mary said. I looked down. The crude clay plate had split into four pieces.

"What's going on here?" I asked.

"You will have to tell me," Cut Mary answered. "At least, you'll have to tell me how you came to this." Mary stepped lightly through the front door. "What a mess," she said.

"I don't even know how I got here."

"That's obvious," Cut Mary said. "Look at the wall, outside. See anything familiar?"

I followed Cut Mary to the stoop and looked around. Trash, debris, broken glass. People living their lives in little loops. Wrecked houses. The door, like all the other doors, was marked in red. A large X, with symbols in each quadrant. A Katrina Cross, but not just any cross. My cross. My hand matched the symbols. This wet wrecked place was my home, and that doll on the sidewalk wasn't made from plastic.

"Mama!" I shrieked. I ran to her. "Mama, I'm sorry, I'm so sorry," I said. I held her and wept. I don't know how long I held her to me, squeezing tight, trying to will life back into her body. Her hair, short and ragged without her wig. I'd seen her float away in the flood. I thought she was the nappy-headed doll. My sister tried to save her, tried to do something, and I didn't.

The neighbors played out their lives again. Then I saw a new thing, a strange thing: a pair of joggers, one older, and one about my age. They wore matching pink Lycra outfits. I'd seen the older woman before, jogging through Northport. Mama. And my sister. Mama and my sister together, alive, healthy, furious.

"Mama?" I asked, still holding her body.

Mama slapped me across the face. "Let go of me!" she shouted. "You got no right to hold me."

"You're alive?"

"You let me die," she said.

"You killed Marcel!" my sister hissed.

"I didn't do anything—"

"You took advantage of him." Mama said.

"I was a child."

"We knew what we were doing," my sister said.

"He deserved to die!" I shouted, so loud my voice flattened the house across the street. "He raped me over and over," I shouted, and my voice ripped the asphalt from the ground. Full of angry tears, I said, "That car pinned him to that fence.

The water rose over his head and I watched. I watched him die. I made sure. I could have saved you Mama, but I had to make sure he died." Thunder shook the ground. I pointed at my sister and Mama. "And I don't give a damn what y'all think. Fuck you, and fuck Marcel!" I howled at the top of my lungs.

I heard a sound, like a dozen doors creaking open. I looked at our house. Thick fingers jammed their way through the X on our door and pulled. I knew those fingers. My body felt those fingers. The door resisted, but he kept pulling at it, insisting, getting his way. I resisted, but every memory of every time he touched me, on my hair, my mouth, my knees, my ass, my nipples, my stomach, my clitoris, my self, all burned at once. The wood started to smolder and I thought I would catch on fire.

Marcel wrenched the wood apart. He stood in the wreckage, bleeding from deep splinters, uncaring. Lumps like blisters or boil had formed across his face. "You mine little mama." He came for me. He walked his strange shuffle walk straight to me, stopped, and knelt. I expected him to say something or try something. Try to touch me again Marcel. Go ahead, try it. I'll kill you. My crossed hand grew warm.

"Can't kill him."

I whirled around and found Cut Mary standing behind us. Mama, Marcel, and my sister stopped moving. "Why not?"

"He's already dead," Cut Mary answered. "You saw him die."

I didn't want to remember. I remembered. I didn't want to remember. I remember.

"You said you made a present for me and this is it?" I demanded. "What would I want with him?"

"Did I say that?" Cut Mary asked. "I didn't make you anything. You made it yourself."

"What are you saying?"

"Look around," Cut Mary said. When I didn't move, she took my head between her hands and moved it. The neighbors repeated their lives again. "Each of them had something to do before they died. They can't move on without help. Can't you do something about it?"

I looked at them repeat their lives over and over, their last moments. The young man wanted to go to work and keep a roof over his family. His wife wanted to feed the baby, and the baby wanted to play. The old men wanted to live out their days among friends. The girl wanted to get home safely. The woman wanted to shoot the man if she had to, but she'd prefer to let him live. He could be hardheaded, but wasn't bad if she went upside his head every now and then. I closed my eyes and felt people moving all through the city, all repeating their last loops, living out unfinished wishes.

"You feel them?" Cut Mary asked. I nodded. "They need you," Cut Mary said. "But family comes first."

"I don't owe them shit," I said.

"Yes Adrian," Cut Mary said gently. "Yes, you do." She let go of me and the scene restarted. I recognized the symbols of the Katrina Cross on my house, ran to the sidewalk and found Mama-the-nappy-headed-doll, argued with my family, and watched Marcel's thick fingers pry the door apart. I recognized the symbols of the Katrina Cross on my house, ran to the sidewalk and found Mama-the-nappy-headed-doll, argued with my family, and watched Marcel's thick fingers pry the door apart. The same thing happened again. I said the same things and they said the same things and we repeated ourselves over and over, living out our own unfinished wishes on one another. Completing their last wish would let them move on.

Fine, I thought. I have a last wish too.

> I signify
>> 10
>> female and male
>>> (but more female)
>> Christian
>>> and
>> Voodoo
>>> and
>> Atheist
>> good luck bad luck no luck
>> health and illness
> Remember to
>> Dismember

Marcel got up from his knees and held me tight. Mama held my head. My twin, angry, gleeful, ice cold, held a pair of sharp scissors like a dagger. I froze in fear. My twin grabbed a bunch of my hair in her hand. She started to hack my hair off.

"You nappy-headed," she declared. "You so ugly."

I cried and screamed, kicked my legs. They wouldn't let go. She wouldn't stop. Clumps of my hair fell to the ground.

"Here you go, honey," my twin said. "I'm gonna take care of you." In her left hand, she held straight blonde hair, the kind used for cheap wigs. In her right, she held a bottle of glue.

I should have screamed, kicked, fought them, but I didn't. All the anger leaked away and left me ashamed. I'd never forgotten this feeling, not for a moment. Me, lying in the dirt, struggling, whispering, begging. I am the girl that is nothing is the girl that is nothing. My twin glued blonde hair onto my head. Globs of glue ran down my head and plugged my ears, glued my eyes shut. Glue got into my nostrils. I started breathing through my mouth, drooling, panting, begging, promising them anything.

"You always want attention," Mama said. "Stop lying."

"Bitch it never happened, you hear me?" Marcel said.

Lying flew up my fingers, up my arm. *Bitch* wriggled past the glue in my ears and slid down frozen canals, fading into the deepest recess, the darkest crevice. Their words slid into my chest, lightless, loveless, hopeless, forgotten. They drew heat from my body into themselves. I grew colder. They dragged me to the yard and dug a shallow trench under the banana tree. They tossed my body into the ditch and covered me with dirt and marked it with trash. My heart slowed, slowed, stopped. Small daisies grew over me. The dirt covering me hardened under the sun. The daisies watched Mama and Marcel and my sister celebrate their lives without me. I shouted for three days. Free Cookie led the Second Line at my funeral parade. The daisies watched the neighbors relive their lives. I dipped my hair in blood and blessed Jackson. I flew down Main Street in slow majesty. I returned and wrecked downtown. I wiggled a toe and a tornado started. I yawned, stretched, and the river jumped its banks. I breathed again and tore rooftops from buildings with the air in my lungs. I rose and looked at the husk of my body in the mud. Mama and Marcel and my sister cowered in the shadows.

You can't hide from me. I can't hide from you.

The people continued their loops. I set the young man's car on its wheels and let him get to work. I fed the baby and played with the baby and let her mother get a nap. I washed the old men, shaved them, cut their hair neatly, dressed them in clean clothes, and set out folding chairs. I escorted the girl home. I raised the gun over the man's head and pulled the trigger until he ran back inside.

I found my family, hiding in the shadows. I embraced Mama and my sister. I accepted them into myself, all their love, their rage, their sorrow, their grief became part of me.

I pushed Marcel away. He moved jerkily, backwards to the front door. He tried to fight, but he was no match for the three of us. I pushed him into the door, into the crack he'd made, feet first. Now he wanted to apologize. He babbled and begged and promised me everything I could ever want if I'd take him back. Money, houses, children. I refused to hear him. I crammed him into the door again and drew the crack closed. I sealed the Katrina Cross, then erased the mark from my home.

I turn grief to life. I turn no way into someway. I give birth and eat the sun and sleep and dream of giving birth and eating the sun give birth and eat the sun and sleep and dream of giving birth and eating the sun give birth and eat the sun and sleep and dream of giving birth and eating the sun give birth and eat the sun and sleep and dream of giving birth and eating the sun give birth and eat the sun and sleep and dream of giving birth and eating the sun give birth and eat the sun and sleep and dream of giving birth and eating the sun give birth and eat the sun and sleep and dream of giving birth and eating the sun.

Cut Mary embraced me. I held her. I said, "We're not in New Orleans."

"We're not in New Orleans."

"We're in Okahika?"

"You are Okahika," she whispered.

Yemaya appeared overhead but I didn't need her. I sang a song I'd heard in a dream of myself.

When she calls, you better follow the sun.
When she calls, you better run, run, run.

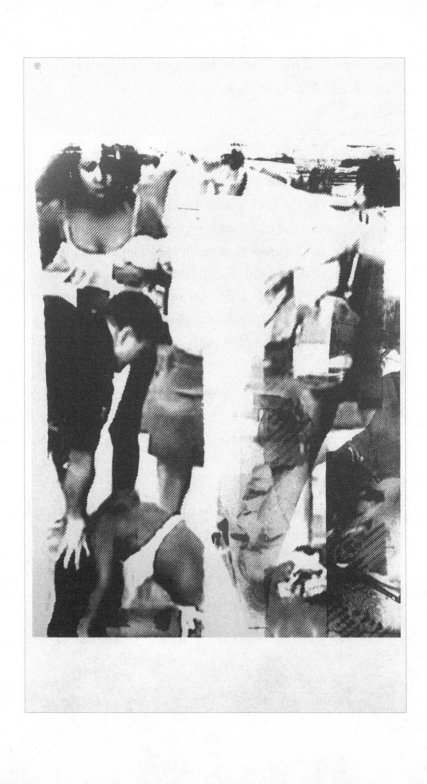

B E N

Epilogue

The baker and the yarn ladies tackled Pats and the Stricklands, took their weapon, and held them until the police arrived. Free Cookie hassled an officer until he thought to follow her and found me clinging onto the fence that led into The Through. I wasn't breathing, and I had broken bones and contusions all over my body. I clung to an old piece of rope. In the hospital, the doctors said only a miracle saved me. I'm an atheist. I don't believe in miracles, but I saw miracles with my own eyes. I am a miracle. I can't reconcile these ideas, the facts and the truth. No rush. They don't have to make sense.

They called it the Great Northport Levee Disaster and said I'd be in the history books, as the lucky survivor. I stayed in the hospital for three weeks. I regained myself, slowly. The doctors bandaged my hands so they could recover from some fierce rope burns. I learned to walk with a new limp that no injection or therapy ever erased. One side neat and orderly; the other side, not quite so.

The doctors told me I could convalesce at home, but I didn't have one. The Chair visited and said that a (real) faculty member on sabbatical had offered his home to me for the next year. The bills were already paid. All I had to do was water the plants. I thanked them both and said yes.

Gloria from Adrian's firm picked me up from the hospital. I broke the news to her—Adrian was gone, and I didn't know if she'd ever come back. Maybe in about 13 years. Gloria looked at me sadly, probably thinking that 'gone' was a euphemism for death, and that Adrian washed away in the flood. That's what everyone believes about Adrian, but not me. I believe that somewhere, somehow, Adrian lives. I asked Gloria if she'd ever heard a bird whose call sounded like 'cheeper-cheeper tape'. She gave me another strange look.

On the way to my new home, I asked Gloria to drive past our old place. I don't know what I thought I'd see. Nothing was left. The crash of *Yemaya* destroyed the house, and the flood washed away what little survived. Except one thing. "Wait here," I said, and then hobbled out of the car. There, in the middle of the yard, stood my peach tree covered in pink blossoms.

The case against Pats and the Stricklands ended in a mistrial. No one could agree on what happened, or why they shot Jackson, or a statue of Jackson, or themselves. I couldn't even sue them. It turned out they had burned through their money, and their investments collapsed. The city took their property in lieu of court costs, condemned it, and eventually tore it down.

I tried to write down what happened: the ship, Adrian, Jackson, Cut Mary, the jogger, Althea, everything, but I skipped all over the place. I wanted a trim and orderly mind, organized like the faculty member's home. I could go to the room with Adrian's name, open the door, and smell her scent. Hear the way she laughed with her entire soul at once. Kiss that one crooked tooth. Dance with her in the kitchen to the Gap Band or Marvin Gaye. Eat lunch together as acquaintances, then friends, then that magic time when love transformed us into new and unanticipated shapes, slowly, word by word, look by look, touch by marvelous touch. The day the waitress assumed we were on a date and neither of them said no. The first night we spent together, drunk with each other. Making love and wondering if I was dreaming. The way my heart skipped a beat every time I saw her. If I could, I would leave all my memories in her room, lower the shades, and quietly but firmly close the door. I could go to the door that said Jackson and hear him brag about himself, and a room with a blue glass door for Cut Mary and a room filled with blooming plants. But my memories look more like the remnants of our house, scattered and broken. I'll have to put them back together, and I'll never get everything exactly right. That's okay too.

A few months later, I attended a wedding. Two of Adrian's old partners, Gloria and Edward tied the knot. They made a cute couple. Edward pulled me aside at the reception and gave me a gift: a keepsake box from Adrian's desk. Pretty feathers, bright beads, things like that. I never knew she collected those. Before they cut the cake, I made my excuses and went home. I think I made people uncomfortable.

At home, I found a package in the mailbox. The return address said C. Mary, Okahika. I opened it. Inside, I found a small book with a red frog over a yellow and white checkerboard cover. The title read *The Mythic Southern: Folktales of Okahika*. I opened the book and a note fell out. I recognized Cut Mary's elegant handwriting.

Past time for an update. - CM

I leafed through the table of contents. The last entry read *Yemaya, by Ben Hughes*. I turned to that page and read the story in one go, especially the parts about Adrian. So that's what happened. I guess I didn't do a bad job writing, but the title didn't work at all.

Late that same night, I made myself a simple dinner of rosemary chicken over a bed of spinach, with a glass of red wine. The cicadas had returned to hibernation, and night fell calm and quiet. A shadow passed over the moon.

I turned NPR on.

NPR interviewed another novelist.

I left the volume on but didn't listen, lost in my own thoughts. Some kinds of love, like some kinds of pain, make us weak. Some kinds make us grow. Others plunge us into deep places. The best writing comes from a deep well of emotion. Some pain, some joy, some regrets. But always from that deep place.

Free Cookie jumped into my lap.

I turned NPR off.

Acknowledgements

Writing your first novel is like swimming underwater while learning to sing whalesong and trying to find a place you've never been to with a map you can't read, while simultaneously writing a novel about swimming underwater while learning to sing whalesong and trying to find a place you've never been to with a map you can't read.

Many amazing people helped me along this journey. Thanks to my family: Mom and Dad, Heather, Heather, Nozomi, Nora, Shiya, and all the Flemings, Johnsons, and Murphys. RIP Scully, my companion and the model for Free Cookie. Also thanks to Juan Reyes, H. Austin Whitver, Mary Meares, Julie Graves, Katie King, Hanne Blank, Yolanda Manora, Michael Martone, Trudier Harris, Casey Clough, and the Kimbilio Center for Fiction.

Art in The Through
was created by
Tomashi Jackson.

Tomashi Jackson was born in Houston, Texas and raised in Los Angeles, California. She holds a MFA in Painting and Printmaking from the Yale School of Art. She earned a degree of Science Master of Art, Culture, and Technology from the M.I.T. School of Architecture and Planning in 2012. She earned her BFA from the Cooper Union School of Art in 2010. Her work has been exhibited in Cambridge, MA., East Lansing, MI., San Francisco, CA., Miami, FL., Minneapolis, MN., and New York City. She has performed at MoMA PS1, Parsons the New School of Design, The Harvard Signet Society, and the Cooper Union for the Advancement of Science and Art. From 2014-present she has organized Game Recognize Game at Yale, apublic speaker series that explores the intersections of art, athletics, visual representation, and non-performance. From 2010-2011 she organized TalkDraw @M.I.T., a public event inviting artists, curators, and technologists to present work to audiences who were encouraged to draw while listening. In 2008 she curated the group shows Publication- Schmublication: publication and dissemination at the Broadway Gallery NYC and Drawing Atmosphere: free-hand drawings by architecture students at Superfront architectural exhibition space in Brooklyn, NY. She has apprenticed for public muralists in the San Francisco Bay Area. Her 20ft x 80ft mural Evolution of a Community was funded by the Los Angeles Department of Cultural Affairs and chronicled in the Los Angeles Times. Jackson is an experienced visual arts educator, facilitating students aged 7-19 years in California and New York at Oakland Technical High School, Performing Arts Workshop San Francisco, Theater of Hearts: Youth First Los Angeles, K.Anthony School, The Buckley School, and Harlem School for the Arts. Her work has been featured in BOMBLOG, The Harvard Crimson, The Yale Daily News, The Yale Herald, and Art Papers.

www.tomashijackson.com

CPSIA information can be obtained
at www.ICGtesting.com
Printed in the USA
BVHW030719250623
666342BV00006B/419